SEAN ROSEN
IS NOT FOR SALE

Jeff Baron

GREENWILLOW BOOKS
An Imprint of HarperCollins*Publishers*

Sean Rosen Is Not for Sale
Copyright © 2014 by Jeff Baron

All rights reserved. No part of this book may be used or reproduced in any manner whatsoever without written permission except in the case of brief quotations embodied in critical articles and reviews. Printed in the United States of America. For information address HarperCollins Children's Books, a division of HarperCollins Publishers, 10 East 53rd Street, New York, NY 10022.
www.harpercollinschildrens.com

The text of this book is set in 12-point Bruce Old Style.
Book design by Paul Zakris

Library of Congress Cataloging-in-Publication Data

Baron, Jeff, (date)
Sean Rosen is not for sale / Jeff Baron.
"Greenwillow Books."
pages cm
Sequel to: I represent Sean Rosen.
Summary: Thirteen-year-old Sean continues to work on his screenplay while juggling seventh grade, track practice, a dog-walking job, recording his podcasts, and trying to keep his movie idea a secret from his parents and a spy sent by a Hollywood movie studio.
ISBN 978-0-06-218750-5 (hardback)
[1. Motion picture industry—Fiction. 2. Middle schools—Fiction. 3. Schools—Fiction. 4. Private investigators—Fiction. 5. Jews—United States—Fiction. 6. Humorous stories.] I. Title.
PZ7.B26889Sed 2014
[Fic]—dc23   2013045849

14 15 16 17 18 CG/RRDH 10 9 8 7 6 5 4 3 2 1
First Edition

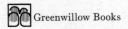 Greenwillow Books

This book is dedicated to my readers,
and to Sean Rosen, who makes my job so easy.

chapter 1

I'm late.

Buzz wanted to check out a new keyboard at the music store, and I wanted a donut, so we decided to meet in fifteen minutes. That was twenty minutes ago.

I had my donut (Boston cream—so good) and got one for Buzz, but then I had five minutes left, which felt like long enough to look around the used bookstore.

Unfortunately, the lady there recognized me.

"Hey, you're the boy who was looking for a book about movies."

"About *making* movies."

"Right. Make any movies yet?"

I *haven't* made any movies yet. But one of the big Hollywood studios *did* want to buy my movie idea. Seriously. They sent me a contract. 10,000 dollars right away, and 40,000 more if the movie got made.

You might think I'm crazy, but I said no. Which means now I have to try not to think about what I would do if I had the money. The new phone I would have, the new computer, the iPad. See? It's not easy. But I think I made the right decision.

For the next five minutes, the used-book lady told me a lot of things about growing zucchini. She's one of those people who doesn't stop between sentences. You never get a chance to say, "I have to go."

Finally someone came into the store and I could leave. I texted Buzz that I was on my way. I hate to be late.

ME: Here's your donut. Sorry
         I'm late.
BUZZ: You're not late.
ME: Yes I am.

BUZZ:	No. You're not late until five minutes after the time.
ME:	I never heard of that. Are you sure?
BUZZ:	You didn't have to text me. I saw you coming.
ME:	How could you see me? I was two blocks away.
BUZZ:	No one else walks like that.
ME:	Like what? I was hurrying.
BUZZ:	You're always hurrying.
ME:	No I'm not.
BUZZ:	Right. Sometimes you stop and just stand there.
ME:	Because I'm thinking. Why? Do you always walk the same speed?

The next day after school, Ethan and I were standing outside on the steps. Well, on different steps. Ethan is about two feet taller than me, and it's a lot easier to talk this way.

"Do I walk funny?"

He thought about it for a second.

"Yeah."

"I *do*?"

"Yeah. So do I. So does everyone. Look."

He's right. Everyone has a funny walk. Everyone's arms look funny when they swing. That kid walks like he's in a race, possibly a race to the bathroom. That girl is walking and texting. She's approaching a tree. Look up! Look up! Ow.

She's okay. She's picking up her phone. She's walking. She's finishing her text.

"Thanks, Ethan."

Good. I'm too busy to worry about how I look when I walk. I have to get home and work on my screenplay for *A Week with Your Grandparents*. That's the movie I decided not to sell to Hollywood.

It's about this brother and sister, Chris and Chloe. He's fifteen and she's twelve. Their parents go away and they're stuck staying with you-know-who. Then they find out that Grandpa invented a virtual reality time machine that lets you spend time with someone on any day in their past. It's so cool. Chris and Chloe meet their grandparents when they were teenagers. The movie is sometimes funny and sometimes scary. The reason I didn't sell it was because I found out the studio wouldn't let me write it. It had to be an experienced screenwriter. Even though it was my idea.

I like most movies, but every once in a while, I hate one. I looked up some movies I hated, and guess what. They were all written by experienced screenwriters. I like this idea too much to let it be a movie I might hate.

I got home, and the painters were getting ready to leave. They've been painting the inside of our house. My parents are both at work, so the painter gave me our key.

"Here you go. All done. We left all the windows open in the family room. Stay out of there for a couple of hours. It'll be dry by then."

"Okay."

I stood in the kitchen and looked at the family room. They painted it last because we couldn't decide on a color. My dad wanted Club Room. You have no idea what color that is, right? How could you? It's dark green. I didn't like it. Neither did my mom.

She wanted Blush. She kept telling my dad and me, "It isn't pink. It's more of a . . . peach." First of all, I wouldn't call peach "not pink." Second, I don't want a pink family room. Neither does my dad.

I wanted it to be blue. I showed them seventeen blues that I liked. Any one of them would have been fine. But my mom and dad aren't "whatever Sean wants" kind of parents. I get one vote, just like everyone else. Blue got a total of one vote.

"Club Room wins. It's a combination of your two colors."

"Sorry, Dad. Green is not a combination of blue and pink."

"Blush *isn't* pink."

We ended up with Biscuit. It's light tan. I'm looking at it right now. It looks good. Thank goodness.

I dropped off my books upstairs. I thought about doing my homework, but I really want to see what happens next in my screenplay. That's what writing it feels like. Like I'm at the movies seeing it, then I just write down what I see. I don't know how it works, but I'm glad it does.

The place I like to work on my screenplay is the family room. Especially when no one else is there. When I write down what the people in the movie are saying, I actually say it out loud. If someone else is in the room, they think I'm talking to them, and they answer. It's distracting.

My parents don't know about this screenplay. They know I'm sort of creative. They know about my podcasts. They're the ones who pay for my subscription to *The Hollywood Reporter*. But they don't know I already started my career in show business. I thought about asking them whether I should sell my movie idea, but I didn't. They don't know the business. My dad is a plumber and my mom is a nurse. Dan Welch thinks I can write the screenplay. He's my manager.

I brought my laptop downstairs and took another look at the family room. I saw that I could definitely make it to the sofa without touching any walls. I *did* make it. I sat on the sofa and wrote for about a half hour.

I don't know why, but writing always makes me hungry. I got up and went to the kitchen to get a snack. I was still thinking about the screenplay, and I suddenly knew what happens next.

I turned to go back to my laptop to write it down, and a rug was where it usually isn't. I slipped and grabbed the wall so I wouldn't fall. He was right. The paint is still wet.

Now right in the middle of our beautiful new wall painted Biscuit is a perfect outline of my hand. If this was a TV detective show, it would be over in twenty seconds.

I wonder if I can fix it. I went to the garage, and I found a can of Biscuit the painters left. Maybe I can put my hand in the paint, then press it on the handprint on the wall.

Maybe not.

My parents still have a paper address book. I looked under P and found the painter's number. I called him and told him what happened. I said

I would pay him if he could come over and fix it before my parents got home. He said okay. I hope I have enough money.

He got here, looked at the wall, and got to work. I kept thinking of different ways to say "I'm sorry," but they all sounded stupid, so I didn't say anything. Also, I don't want to interrupt him. He probably gets paid by the hour.

It took him about twenty minutes. It looks perfect. I finally got the courage to say, "How much?"

"Are you going to listen next time when I tell you to stay out of the room?"

"Yes." I actually think I will.

"Okay. Yesterday you offered me lemonade without anyone telling you to. We're even."

chapter 2

My parents got home, and they both like the color of the family room. I didn't tell them about my little accident, but I also didn't try to stand in front of the place on the wall where my hand landed. We decided to go out for supper, because my mom said, "Anything we eat here is going to taste like paint. Not Biscuits."

I heard that I got a text during dinner, but we have a "no devices at the table" rule in our family, so I waited until we got back into the car to look.

Dug wants 2 no wot dave mots sez

It's Buzz. And it's not just texting language. Buzz can't spell. He's telling me that Doug (not Dug), who plays drums in Buzz's band, wants to know what Dave Motts (not Mots) thinks about the band's MP3.

If I heard anything from Dave Motts, I would have told them. Buzz knows that. I'm sure Doug made him send that text.

Doug and I used to be friends, but then he did something really mean to me, and a year later, I did something really mean to him. Then we didn't really talk anymore. Well, *I* didn't talk. He kept saying nasty things to me, which was actually a little scary. Doug was always one of the biggest kids, and last year he suddenly got a lot bigger.

But lately Doug has been acting a lot nicer to me. He thinks I can help the band. The band, for some strange reason, is called Taxadurmee. I asked Buzz about it.

ME: Why did you pick that name?
           It's creepy.
BUZZ: No it's not. It's cool.
ME: Do you know what it means?
BUZZ: No. No one does.
ME: *I* do. It means stuffing dead

	animals so you can put them on your wall.
BUZZ:	No it doesn't.
ME:	Look it up.
BUZZ:	*You* look it up.

Anyway, Taxadurmee recorded two songs (that's all they have so far), and they sent me the MP3 to give to Dave Motts. They're hoping he'll like the songs, want to be their manager, get them a record contract, and make them rich and famous.

Dave Motts isn't a real person. Well, there may be a real person named Dave Motts, but the Dave Motts that Taxadurmee is waiting to hear from doesn't exactly exist. It's a long story.

It started when I tried to tell Buzz about the big movie studio wanting to buy my movie. That was a disaster. First, Buzz never heard of the studio, which is impossible. If you ever watched TV or ever went to the movies, you've heard of this studio. Seriously, *everyone* knows them.

I also told him about my manager, Dan Welch. I even said, "Welch, like the grape juice." Then, even though I told Buzz not to tell anyone about the movie or Dan Welch, he told Doug, except he said my manager's name is Dave (not Dan) Motts (like the *apple* juice). Anyway, now Buzz and Doug want "Dave Motts" to listen to their songs, so maybe he'll want to manage them too.

You're probably thinking Buzz is kind of dumb. He actually isn't. He just doesn't really pay attention. It's like his songs are playing in his head all the time, so he can't really hear anything else, including my manager's name.

Dan Welch . . . Dave Motts. It doesn't actually matter. Neither one of them is going to listen to that MP3. They can't. Neither of them is a real person.

I *had* to make up Dan Welch. The big companies in Hollywood won't even talk to you unless you have an agent or a manager. I learned this the hard way. I wrote a letter to one of the big studios, and their legal department sent me a six-page letter telling me to stay away from them until I have an agent or a manager.

I tried to get an agent. I tried to get a manager.

I couldn't. No one wanted to represent me. Then I thought up Dan Welch. His name came from our refrigerator. Dan from Dannon yogurt and Welch from Welch's grape juice.

I got him an email address, and when Dan Welch wrote to that same gigantic Hollywood studio that wouldn't talk to me, suddenly they wanted to talk to me. Soon they wanted to buy my movie idea. He turned out to be a very good manager.

I know it's me who actually writes Dan Welch's emails and chats, but even to me he feels like a separate person. I don't know what he looks like, but I know he's a little older than my parents, and he has kids.

He and I are so completely different. He never acts like a thirteen-year-old. Unfortunately, I usually do. His feelings don't get hurt as easily as mine. And he can say nice things about me that I would never say about myself.

Wait. I'll give you an example. Here's the email Dan Welch sent to Hank Hollywood (not his real name), the Chairman of the huge entertainment company that I want to work with on this other idea of mine. I think they're the best company for it, because they're in so many different parts of the entertainment business. By the way, Chairman is actually a higher job than President. Hank Hollywood's company has a bunch of different Presidents.

To: Hank Hollywood
From: Dan Welch Management

Dear Hank,

I represent Sean Rosen. He recently turned down an offer from Stefanie V. President (not her real name) at _____ (the name of her studio) to buy his movie *A Week with Your Grandparents*. Sean is currently writing the screenplay.

You may be familiar with Sean's podcasts, which he writes and produces. Some of them are available online. He's accomplished a lot for a thirteen-year-old.

Sean asked me to contact you because he has a very

interesting idea. It's not an idea for a movie or a TV show. It's a whole new way of making and selling movies and TV shows, as well as games and theater. As Sean puts it, "I think it will change the way people think about entertainment."

I know that's hard to picture, but it was also hard to picture a major Hollywood studio wanting to buy a movie idea from a kid they never heard of before.

Sean has a lot of respect for your company, and you're his first choice for working together on his big idea. If you're interested, please let me know, and I'll be glad to set up a meeting for you and Sean on Skype.

Best,
Dan

I couldn't have written that letter for myself. I'd be too nervous. I would never say, "You may be familiar with Sean's podcasts." I *know* Hank Hollywood has never seen my podcasts.

Why would he just decide one day to go to www.SeanRosen.com or YouTube and watch podcasts by some kid he never heard of? Dan Welch said that so Hank Hollywood would *want* to watch them.

By the way, Dan Welch used Stefanie V. President's real name and her studio's name in the actual letter. They all know each other out there, or at least that's what it feels like when you see them on award shows and talk shows.

You probably want to know what my idea is. Unfortunately, I can't tell you. Yet. I will, I promise. Or else you'll just hear about it and start using it, because Hank Hollywood's company decided to take it. But I can't tell you now, because I think it's worth a lot of money, and even if you didn't try to steal it, it's such a cool idea that you'd definitely tell someone about it, and *that* person might steal it.

I had this idea, my big idea, before I ever thought of *A Week with Your Grandparents*. Dan Welch and I were just practicing on Stefanie's studio with a movie idea. But then when they actually wanted to buy it, we stopped working on the big idea. I'm not sorry we did that, because I think we learned a lot about the business.

Anyway, while I write the screenplay, Dan Welch can concentrate on the big idea. I want to get it sold before someone else thinks of it. I'm actually surprised that didn't happen yet.

That's why I got a separate email address for Dave Motts. Dave can work on music while Dan Welch helps me sell the big idea. I don't exactly know *how* Dave Motts is going to work on music, but I'll figure it out. I have to. Doug isn't going to be nice to me forever.

Now if you were Hank Hollywood and you got that letter from Dan Welch . . . wouldn't you want to know who Sean Rosen is, and what his big idea is? Why didn't he write back? Doesn't the Chairman usually want his company to make more money? I'm sure he's busy, but it's been five whole days.

chapter 3

I think I'm on the school track team. I always thought if you wanted to be on a team, you had to try out. I didn't have to. Today, at the end of phys ed, Mr. Obester stopped me on the way to the locker room. I thought he was going to yell at me because I didn't play rugby. There are a couple of places in our gym where you can hide, and usually they're taken, but today I got one.

"Sean, I want to talk to you about something."

"Sorry about rugby today, but—"

"This isn't about rugby. I need you on my track team."

"Me? *Need?*"

"Yeah, I saw how you aced the mile in the

President's Challenge. You're going to be my new miler. Big meet next week."

"Like a real track meet?"

"Yeah. A real track meet. Next Tuesday after school."

"All I have to do is run a mile?"

"That's it. I mean, you'll come to track practice the rest of this week and train."

"When you say 'train,' what do you mean exactly?"

"Oh, it's fun. Just running around . . . a few exercises. Maybe a game."

"What kind of game?"

"A running game. You're gonna love it."

"Okay. Do I need to bring anything?"

He reached into his pocket. "Just get one of your parents to sign this permission slip."

"What do I wear?"

"Just gym clothes for practice. We'll get you a uniform for the meet."

"A uniform? Really? So I'm actually on the team?"

"You actually are. See you here after school tomorrow."

I went home and had a snack, did some homework, went for a bike ride, and looked at Dan Welch's empty inbox about 200 times. Then I came downstairs for dinner. My mom was asking my dad about his day.

MOM: I thought you already fixed their toilet.

DAD: I did. This was a different one. These people have a lot of toilets.

MOM: Was it really broken, or did she just want a little more alone time with the hot plumber?

DAD: It was really broken.

MOM: Interesting. She figured out how to break toilets. What was she wearing?

DAD: I was looking at her

toilet, not *her.*

MOM: So you didn't even notice. . . .

DAD: You couldn't *not* notice. How about *you?*

MOM: How about me *what?*

DAD: Don't guys pretend they're still sick so you can keep being their nurse?

MOM: No.

DAD: No?

MOM: Yes.

I had enough of this conversation.

ME: Can one of you sign this?

I handed them the permission slip. They looked at it together.

ME: Do you want me to get your glasses?

MOM: No.

DAD: No.

They both pretend they don't need glasses. I
don't know why, but the farther away from their
eyes they hold it, the easier it is for them to read.
My dad held the permission slip. He has longer
arms.

MOM: You made the track team?
            Nice. I didn't know you
            tried out.
ME: I didn't. They just want me
            to run in a race next week.
DAD: Because of the President's
            thing?
ME: Exactly.
DAD: Cool.
MOM: Do you want to?
ME: I guess.
MOM: Good. Anything that'll get
            you outside.
ME: I go outside.
MOM: Occasionally.

DAD:	He rides his bike a lot.
MOM:	A *lot*?
ME:	Who wants to sign it?
DAD:	I will. Your mom might miss the dotted line.

My parents like to tease each other (and me sometimes), but they really like each other. A lot. I feel sorry for my friends whose parents fight all the time. Like Brianna.

I know her parents fight all the time because she tells me. I've actually never seen her parents together. I met her mom a few times, and last week I finally met her dad.

I went over to Brianna's house after school to work on our math homework together. Well, I was going to work on it, and she was going to copy it when I was done.

Brianna thinks math is obsolete. "There's probably an app for it, and if not, your accountant or your business manager or your husband will take care of it."

This is the first time I ever heard Brianna say the word "husband." I don't know why, but I thought that growing up in a house where your parents always fight would make you not want to get married.

I was sitting alone in her kitchen working on the math. She was on the phone talking to one of her many girlfriends. When I asked who it was, she decided she needed privacy, and she went to another room. It's a huge house, so there are a lot of choices.

A few minutes later, her dad walked into the kitchen. I knew it was her dad because he looks like Brianna. Her mom doesn't, but maybe that's because she keeps getting things changed on her face.

It's a big kitchen, so he didn't see me at first. Then he did.

"Who are you?"

"Sean. I'm Brianna's friend."

"Whose kid are you?"

"I don't think you know my parents."

"How do *you* know who I know?"

"I don't, actually. Do you know Jack and Elise Rosen?"

"No."

"See?"

He just looked at me for a second. "Whatever you're doing here . . ."

"Math."

". . . how about doing it somewhere else?"

"Oh. Sure. Okay."

I got up, and I quickly put my homework in my backpack and walked out the door. When I got outside, I didn't know what to do. I know Brianna was counting on getting that homework from me. I guess I can finish it at home, then scan it and email it to her. I felt a little bad leaving without saying good-bye, but her dad is scary.

I looked around, and suddenly I was very confused. I never came in or went out Brianna's kitchen door before. I didn't know whether to go left or right or straight ahead.

If this was my house, it would be easy. We have two doors, and if you walk out the back door, you can go left or right, just follow along the house, and in a few seconds, you're at the front door. But here, everything is really, really big.

First I turned right and walked along the house. After a while, I came to a big locked gate. I kept looking for a way to open it, but I guess they really don't want you to get in (or out).

Then I walked in the other direction. When I passed the kitchen door, I ducked down so Brianna's dad wouldn't see me.

I kept walking, but the house just went on and on. I finally got to the end of it, but there were all these tall bushes with gigantic thorns. You couldn't walk through them. Farther down were some woods. I thought maybe I could find a way back to the street.

There was something that sort of looked like a path, but then it turned out it wasn't one. It's all just gigantic trees. I looked in every direction, but I couldn't see the house anymore. This was getting scary. How can you not see a house as big as Brianna's?

Suddenly I heard a dog barking. Really loud.

At first I thought, "Oh, good. They sent a search party." I was just about to start yelling, but then I thought, "What if it's a wild dog with rabies? What if it's some other forest animal that only *sounds* like a very loud dog?"

Then I remembered my phone. I forgot I had it. I texted Brianna.

    S: I'm lost in the forest.

    B: Forest? What r u talking about?

    S: Outside your house.

    B: Why r u outside?

    S: Your dad told me to leave.

    B: No he didn't.

    S: Yes he did.

    B: Did u finish the math?

    S: No. He told me to leave before I could finish.

    B: :-(

    S: I'm really lost. Can u come get me?

    B: I'm on the phone. Where r u?

    S: Go out the kitchen door, turn left, and walk into the woods.

    B: No way. I'll send my dad.

    S: NOOOO!!!!

Brianna's dad found me. He was really mad. "When I told you to go somewhere else, I didn't mean go snooping all over my property."

"Sorry."

"I meant go to a different room."

"Sorry."

"I wanted to use my kitchen. There are lots of other rooms in this house you could have gone to."

"Sorry. I should actually get going. Can you give me directions to the front door?"

chapter 4

Finally! Something came for Dan Welch. It wasn't from Hank Hollywood, but in a way, it's even better. I think.

To: Dan Welch Management
From: Stefanie V. President

Dan! How are you? I miss you! I miss Sean. How is he? I'm guessing he's discovering how hard it is to write a screenplay. I tried once. As you know, it's a residency requirement here in L.A.

I got a funny phone call from Hank Hollywood. (She used his real name.) Did you know I started out in the business as his intern? Not an easy job, by the way. Marisa is now three months old, and last night, after hours and hours of feeding her, changing her, and rocking her, I thought, "Who do you remind me of?" Hank Hollywood! He wants what he wants when he wants it, and if he doesn't get it, he starts screaming.

Hank asked me about Sean. I know you threatened to go to them when I told you we'd need to bring in a screenwriter for *A Week with Your Grandparents*, but Hank doesn't seem to know anything about the movie. He *wants* to know, but I'm not telling him. Were you just testing the waters? Or does Sean have *another* movie idea???

As I told you back then, no one will ever let Sean write a big Hollywood feature. Even if Hank says he will, I guarantee you he'll have a real screenwriter writing it at the same time. I know how he operates, and I would hate for Sean (or you) to get your hopes up.

We still love the idea, and if Hank makes an offer, I

hope you'll let me know. I don't know if you watch *The Voice*, but remember, I pushed my button first!

I may even be able to sweeten the pot a little, but I still can't hire Sean as a screenwriter. I actually ran it by the big cheese, and as I suspected, he laughed and said no.

If you need me to deconstruct anything Hank Hollywood promises you, don't hesitate to call or write. I'm his only ex-intern who's still in the business.

Tell Sean I send him a big hug, and please remind him that my door is always open to him. I want to hear any and every idea he has.

Dan, you know the kinds of movies we do here. Let me know if any of your other clients (they don't have to be adolescents) have something you think I'll like.

Best,
Stefanie

That's so cool! The Chairman of maybe the biggest entertainment company in the world called the Vice President of one of the other biggest entertainment companies in the world to talk about ME. Dan Welch, you've done it again.

I've actually been mad at Stefanie V. President since she said I couldn't write my own movie, but her email reminds me how nice she is. I only met her on Skype, but still. Her door is always open to me.

I had to look up a few things she said. She said she'd help us "deconstruct" what Hank Hollywood promises. I think she's saying she can tell us what he really means. I wish I had someone to help me deconstruct the fifty-page contract that Stefanie's business affairs department sent me for *A Week with Your Grandparents*. I ended up not signing it.

When she said she might be able to "sweeten the pot," I think she means she can pay me more money for *A Week with Your Grandparents*. She already sweetened the pot once. At first they offered me only 500 dollars, but then when Dan Welch complained, they changed it to 10,000 dollars.

I wonder how sweet she would make the pot. It doesn't really matter if they still won't let me write the screenplay. Does it? What if she offered us a million dollars?

I went downstairs. My parents were still in the kitchen, cleaning up after dinner. My dad was doing the dishes. Whoever makes dinner, the other one cleans up. My mom was finishing her glass of wine.

ME: **What would you do if I gave you a million dollars?**

I'm not saying I'd give it to them, at least not all of it, but I wanted to hear what they'd say.

DAD: **I'd get my van painted.**

MOM: **You wouldn't just get a new van?**

DAD: **No. I like my van.**

MOM: **Except for the color?**

DAD: No. I like the color. I'm
           getting tired of that
           slogan.
ME: Finally.

I'm not going to tell you the slogan because
my dad's a good guy, and I want you to like him.
Everyone makes bad jokes sometimes, but when it's
a plumbing joke, and it's on your van, it's worse.

ME: So if you had a million
           dollars, you'd keep working?
DAD: Definitely.
MOM: Jack, we can just paint
           over that slogan. You don't
           need a million dollars.
           Let's do it right now.
ME: Mom, would *you* keep
           working?
MOM: (to me) Absolutely.
           (to my dad) Are you done?
           I know a paint store that's
           still open.

Okay, forget the million dollars. My parents don't even want it. Maybe Stefanie and "the big cheese" at her studio will find out I actually *can* write a screenplay.

Hank Hollywood didn't say anything about my big idea to Stefanie. And she won't tell him what *A Week with Your Grandparents* is about. I guess I'm not the only one who keeps secrets.

chapter 5

After I woke up, I stayed under the covers for a few minutes. Why am I so nervous? It's only track practice. Whatever that is. I really have no idea what they do. What *we* do. I guess I'm on the team now. I wonder who else is on the track team. Is it boys and girls together?

Do people actually come to watch middle-school track meets? A lot of people? Will having a bunch of people watching me make me run faster . . . or slower? What if they start cheering? Will that make me want to win even more? Or will I start worrying that everyone who's cheering for me will hate me if I lose?

At least I'm not worrying about Hank Hollywood

writing back to Dan Welch. Now that I know he called Stefanie to ask about me, I have a feeling we'll hear from him soon.

We got a fun assignment in English today. We have to do an interview with a character in the book we're reading. You ask them questions and then you imagine how they would answer. I like to do interviews. I don't know if you ever saw my podcasts (www.SeanRosen.com), but they're mostly interviews.

I doubt Miss Meglis, our English teacher, ever saw my podcasts. I don't talk about them much at school. When things are on the internet, you don't know who looks at it. It would be fun to know.

Actually, maybe it wouldn't, because if you knew that someone watched your podcast and then you saw them and they didn't say anything about it, you would think they hated it. But you might be wrong. Maybe they started it, but then they got interrupted and didn't really watch it, even though your List of Watchers says they did.

I keep wanting to ask kids in my class if they're on the track team, but I have no idea who to ask.

Maybe after English, I'll ask my friend Javier. He's good at sports. I think he's actually the star of the soccer team. He moved here last year from Argentina. For some reason, people from Argentina are better at soccer than we are.

"Javi, are you on the track team?"

"No. I want to be, but I got my extra English class after school."

"You *have* your extra English class after school." He always wants me to correct him.

"I *have* my extra English class after school. Why, amigo?"

"Oh. Coach Obester sort of asked me to be on the team." I never called Mr. Obester "Coach" before, but I've heard kids on teams do it.

"Cool, Sean. You the man."

"*You're* the man."

"No. *You're* the man. Running, no?"

"*Sí.*"

"You're fast. I remember. Hey, Doug! Guess what?"

NO! I don't want everyone to know I'm on the track team until I'm sure I actually am. Mr.

Obester might change his mind. And Doug is the last person I would tell. He's on the football team, and he always makes fun of me. In fact, the reason I ran the mile so fast in the President's Challenge was because I was running away from Doug. In fact, Doug might even be on the track team. Not running, but maybe throwing something. He's strong. At least he looks strong.

"What?"

"Sean's on the track team."

"He is?" I've known Doug since we were five years old. He was about to say something really mean, but then you could see him stop and remember that I might be helping Taxadurmee get a recording contract. "Good."

I made myself talk to him. "Doug, are *you* on the track team?"

"Nah." You could see him think of what he wanted to say and then not say it. But then he couldn't help it. "I'm on *real* teams. Football and baseball."

Javier said, "Track is real. The Olympics."

"Right. Sorry, Sean. Hope you win a gold medal.

When are you going to hear something from Dave Motts?"

"He's very busy, Doug. As soon as I hear something I'll let you know."

"Whatever."

There are places in my school where I feel completely comfortable. Like Miss Meglis's English class. Like the Publication Room (I'm one of the yearbook editors). My other comfortable place will sound strange, because for a lot of kids it's the scariest place in the whole school. The principal's office. As in "Go to the principal's office! Right now!"

I actually did get sent to the principal's office that way. It *was* scary. Especially the first time. But then I got to know the principal a little. Mr. Parsons is tough, but I think he's fair. He listens when you tell him why you did whatever stupid thing you did. Sometimes he punishes you, but not by yelling at you in front of everyone. He takes away something you like.

My parents try to do that too, but he's better at

it than they are. When he gives you a punishment, he never changes it. If you get caught using your phone during school, then for a whole week you have to give him your phone when you get to school. One kid gave Mr. Parsons his phone, but the next day he brought another phone, and when he got caught using it, Mr. Parsons took that one too. He wouldn't give either of them back until the kid's parents came in. They ended up taking him out of our school. I guess now he's in a school where they let you use your phone.

Mr. Parsons's assistant is named Trish, and she's one of my favorite people at the school. I like to visit her sometimes. She's smart and she's funny, and she knows how everything works at our school. If there's ever a nuclear attack, and for some reason it happens at our school, she's the person I would follow. That probably won't happen.

TRISH: Hey, Sean. How was your day?

ME: Oh. Pretty good. You know . . .

TRISH: No. I *don't* know. Tell me.

ME: Oh. It's just that I'm
           supposed to go to this . . .
           track team practice.

TRISH: You're *supposed* to?

ME: Yeah. I mean I'm actually
           going. I think. I'm just a
           little nervous.

TRISH: That's good. You'll run
           better. Get going.

So I did.

chapter 6

I got to the locker room. They give us a little locker where we can keep our gym clothes. There are signs all over the locker room that say WASH YOUR GYM CLOTHES. I do wash them, or actually my mom does, whenever I bring them home. But maybe it's been a few weeks.

When Mr. Obester told me I was on the team, I didn't have time to come to the gym to see how they smell. So I brought other stuff just in case. My gym clothes smell okay. Not great. I guess I'll wear the ones I brought. As I was changing, some other kids came in. I can't tell if they're here for track practice or for some other team. I sort of know a lot of the kids in my school because of the yearbook. I'm there when they get their picture taken, then I do layouts of their pictures in the actual e-yearbook.

A few people said hi to me, but they had this look on their faces like "What are *you* doing here?" No one actually said that, but I could tell, because I was thinking the same thing. About myself, I mean.

I went out the door everyone else was going out, which takes you outside. Mr. Obester was there with about 25 kids, all boys. He blew his whistle, but not so it hurt your ears. Just loud enough for everyone to hear. I never heard anyone do that before.

"Guys . . . this is Sean Rosen." He took the permission slip I was holding and looked at it for a second. "He's our new miler. Okay, let's go."

Suddenly everyone started running around the track. Every single kid except me. Then Mr. Obester did another one of those quiet whistles. He pointed to the track, and I started running after everybody.

I caught up to them pretty quickly, then I started

passing a lot of kids. I guess I actually am a good runner. It was exciting. I was just passing another kid when I heard him say, "Warm-up run." Oh. This isn't a race.

I like this track. It's made of something like rubber, so it's bouncy when you run. You feel like if you jumped, you might be able to fly up in the air and land in front of everyone else. I wanted to try it, even if this isn't a race, but I decided not to.

We made it around the track once, then Mr. Obester said, "Runners keep going." Some of the kids stopped running, and I actually felt like stopping too, but I guess I'm a runner now, so I kept going. I was still next to the kid who told me it was only a warm-up run. I think his name is Brandon, but I'm not sure.

"How many more times do we have to do this?"

"*Too* many times." Then we ran a little more. "You're a miler, so you have to do even more laps than me."

"What are you?"

"I'm a sprinter."

I started thinking about asking Mr. Obester if I could be a sprinter instead of a miler, but then I thought I better ask Might-Be-Brandon another question.

"What do the sprinters have to do?"

"Sprints and sprints and *more* sprints. It's killer."

"How long does practice actually last?"

"We have a big meet next week, so he'll keep us here right until five."

"Another hour and fifteen minutes?"

"Yeah."

"Is there like a rest period?"

"Not really."

"Mr. Obester said part of practice was playing a game."

"I hope not. The games are the worst."

I was starting to get a little tired and a little bored. I thought about sitting on the couch in my family room drinking lemonade and working on my screenplay. That's what I would be doing right now if I wasn't on the track team.

When am I going to work on my screenplay? I

want to finish it while Stefanie V. President still loves the idea. If I have to run like this every day after school, I won't have time. I'll come home from track, eat supper, do my homework, and fall asleep. I feel like sleeping right now.

But I'm the new miler. Coach wants me on the track team. He *needs* me. I see him working with some of the other kids. They're doing pushups. Is that next?

We got back to where we started, and Mr. Obester yelled, "Sprinters, come with me. Everyone else, keep going."

Might-Be-Brandon and some other kids stopped, and six of us kept going. Well, five of us. I stopped and walked over to Mr. Obester.

"One more lap, Sean."

"Mr. Obester . . . can I talk to you for a second?"

"Sure. Call me Coach."

"Coach . . . I really want to be your miler."

"You *are* my miler. You're gonna be great."

"Well, I hope so. When's that big meet?"

"Tuesday."

"Okay. Good. Tuesday is good. Would it be okay if . . . between now and Tuesday . . . I just . . . sort of practice on my own?"

"You mean do some extra running on the weekend?"

"Well . . ."

"I like your dedication, but trust me, you'll get enough miles in practice. Give yourself the weekend off."

"Okay. But what I actually meant was, I don't think I can keep coming to track practice."

"Why not?"

"It's just a little too . . . I don't know. . . ."

"It gets easier. It really does."

Might-Be-Brandon made it sound like it really doesn't.

"I just don't think I can."

"You can if you *want* to." I didn't know what to say. "You want to leave *now*?"

"Actually, yeah. But I promise to be there on Tuesday."

"For what?"

"To run the mile."

Mr. Obester didn't say anything. He looked at me for a really long time. The looks on his face kept changing. Some of them were a little scary. Then he smiled.

"Sorry, Sean. It doesn't work that way. It wouldn't be fair to the other guys."

"Okay. Thanks for asking me to run."

"Hit the road."

Fortunately, he was still smiling.

chapter 7

Walking home after track practice, I thought about all the people I'd have to tell that I'm not on the track team anymore.

Javier. He'll feel bad. *"¿Por qué, mi amigo?"* ("Why, my friend?")

Doug. He'll try not to laugh. He'll think of the mean thing he wants to say to me, but he won't say it. I don't know how long that's going to last. If I don't get Dave Motts to listen to that MP3, Doug might actually explode.

What's that smell? Oh. It's my gym clothes. The ones I had in my locker. Maybe they were there a little longer than a few weeks. I left the ones I wore today in my locker. They were only a little sweaty.

Who else? Trish. I only see her once in a while. But she remembers everything. So she'll ask me about the track team, she'll be disappointed for two seconds, then she'll say something that makes me feel good.

Mom and Dad. I guess I'll tell them at dinner. What will I say? "So . . . I decided not to be on the track team." They'll ask me why. They'll remind me that sometimes with new things, I think I don't like it, but then after a little while, I do. That's actually true, but I'll tell them that with this, I'm sure, and that will be it.

I know my parents think I'm a good kid. They trust me. I'm not saying they never get mad at me. They do. And when they do, I don't blame them. *I'd* be mad at me too.

But if my grades aren't the best or if I don't like the same things they like, they don't make me feel bad. They don't compare me to other kids. They're proud of me. They like that I just started doing my podcasts on my own and that I keep doing them.

It would have been nice to let them be proud of me for something normal. They could have said, "Hey! Guess what? Sean's on the track team. He's running the mile in a big meet on Tuesday." Except he's not.

I was feeling a little sad as I turned the corner onto my street. Then Baxter saw me and started barking. Baxter is my neighbors' dog. He loves me and I love him. I went over to say hi, and he jumped on me and licked my face.

We don't have a dog, and I want one, but my mom doesn't. She won't try to talk me into going to track practice tomorrow, and I don't try to talk her into getting a dog. Well, I *did* for about five years, but then I figured out that if she ever changes her mind, she'll tell me.

I played with Baxter for a little while, then I went home and had a snack. I looked at the clock in the kitchen. It's 4:30. If I was at practice, I'd still be running or doing pushups or something like that. I'm going to use the time I saved to work on my screenplay.

I went upstairs to get my laptop. Before getting to work, I checked Dan Welch's email to see if anything came from Hank Hollywood. Something came, but not the way I thought it would.

When I made up the name Dan Welch, I never thought there was someone whose actual name is Dan Welch. This other Dan Welch found my Dan Welch's email address on my website when he was Googling himself. Then he just started writing to my Dan Welch, trying to sell him collectibles and saying nice things about my podcasts.

To: Dan Welch Management
From: Dan Welch

Hey, Dan Welch! Its Dan Welch again. Hows it hangin buddy? You never told me what you want me to call you. DW? Danny Boy? Welchie? I been called all those and worse. I got more nicknames than barfing, but I still dont know yours.

Now that I'm thinking about it, you never did write back to me, did you. R u there Dan Welch?

The reason I'm asking is I got a email that might be for you. Some showbiz thing about your boy Sean Rosen. Tell him i keep checking back for new podcasts. That kids got something. I never went to a Bar Mitts-fa before his Bar Mitts-fa podcast.

Hey! Did you check out my website yet? You remember. UNameItIGotIt.com. I just got in a bunch of cool new collectibles. I don't know how old you are Mr Welch (is THAT what I should call you??), but if your close to my age you defenitely want the original Farrah Fawcett poster. You know the one. With the teeth and the hair and the rest. I wouldn't of made it thru jr high without sweet Farrah on my wall. I just found 2 in mint condition. I'm keeping one, but if you need the other one

(YOU DO), you can have it for less than what I'm asking for it on the website. Its the Dan Welch discount, Dan Welch!

Okay. Gotta go. Get back to me and tell me your the right guy and I'll send you that email about Sean Rosen.

Hey, if Sean is still in touch with the guy in his post office podcast who bought the Willie Mays card, tell him to tell that guy I got some A-Mays-ing Willie merch, and I dont charge as much as whoever he bought that card from.

The Other Dan Welch

I didn't know what a Farrah Fawcett was, but I looked it up and it's a person. She was a pretty actress, and I found the poster Collectibles Dan Welch is talking about. I see what he means.

I wonder who wrote to Collectibles about me.

Not Stefanie. She knows Dan Welch's email address.

Could it be Hank Hollywood? *He* knows Dan Welch's email address too. He has it on the email Dan sent him about my big idea. Wouldn't he just hit reply?

Is it from someone who saw my podcasts and wants me to do something else, or wants to use "I Want a Donut!" for a commercial? No. Because they'd have the right Dan Welch's email address too, from my website.

Did Collectibles just make something up about me so Dan Welch would finally write back to him? Why would he? Maybe he's lonely.

Now I can't work on my screenplay. If I don't find out what that email is about, I'm just going to think about it all the time. I mean *all* the time. Which would be even more distracting than getting more emails from Collectibles Dan Welch.

I'll let my manager handle this.

From: Dan Welch Management

To: Dan Welch

Dear Dan,

Good to hear from you. I'm glad you like Sean's podcasts. I do too.

Yes, please forward that email to me at this address.

Best,

Dan

chapter 8

After school today I got a text from Brianna.

B: We're going to band practice tonight.

S: Who's we?

B: You and me.

S: We are?

B: Yes. We'll pick you up at 7.

S: Who's we?

B: My mom. Unless you think we should take a taxi.

S: My parents are not letting me get in a taxi.

B: Good. Have one of them drive you to my house.
   We can walk to Buzz's from here.

S: Really?

B: What part doesn't sound real?

S: Do they even want us there?

B: Trust me. The two people in the world they want there are you and me.

I had to think about that. They want *me* there, because I'm the one who knows Dave Motts, the guy they think is going to make them rich and famous.

B: For different reasons, of course.

Brianna likes Buzz, and she's pretty sure Buzz likes her. She wants me to ask him, but I won't. I don't want to get in the middle of this. Brianna and Buzz are both my friends, and it's weird enough that they might like each other. Don't make me help.

This started when Taxadurmee did a concert at our school. We never have bands for assembly programs, and then when they turned out to be good, everyone was excited about them. Brianna never saw Buzz before that, because he goes to a different school. I think that's part of what she likes about him. She thinks it's cool to like a boy who doesn't go to our school. He's a year older than us, which she also likes. He's in seventh grade like we are, but he keeps changing schools, and in one of those changes, they made him do a grade over again.

I don't know if I want to go to band practice. I don't like to watch people practice things. I'd rather see it when they're done practicing.

Also, it might make me feel bad. Brianna doesn't know this, but when Buzz first started the band, he asked me to be in it. He wanted me to be the singer, or as he said in his text, the "singger."

I was actually thinking about doing it, but when I heard that Doug was in the band, I said no. Why would I want to spend time with someone who's usually mean to me?

The other reason is that I'm actually not good enough to be in that band. I like to sing, but I'm just okay at it. I couldn't really sing Buzz's songs. Buzz should sing them. He has the right voice for his songs.

Why am I wasting time deciding if I want to go to band practice? I'm going. Brianna will make me.

My mom called Buzz's mom to make sure an adult will be in the house. My mom doesn't really *get* Buzz's mom. In fact, when my mom asked if an adult was going to be there, I don't think she was counting Buzz's mom as an adult.

But my mom likes Buzz (even though she doesn't get *him* either), and she likes that I have friends who want me to come over, plus it's not a school night, so she drove me to Brianna's. She made me put my phone on vibrate so it doesn't interrupt the music, then she made me move it to a pocket where I'll actually feel it when it vibrates. She waited until Brianna opened the door. Then I waved and she drove away.

Brianna came to the door wearing very, very tight jeans, a sparkly T-shirt, and a vest over the T-shirt.

"Are you *auditioning* for the band?"

She ran upstairs to change and left me at the front door. I didn't know what to do. This is my first time at the house since that time with Brianna's dad. I wonder if he's home.

"Are there more of you coming?" It's him. What does he mean? "Why else would you leave the door open?"

"Oh. No. *I* didn't. Brianna did."

"But you could have closed it."

"Oh. Sorry." If I closed it, he'd probably yell at me for touching his door.

"Am I supposed to drive you two somewhere?"

"No. We don't need a ride. It's close. Thanks anyway."

He walked away.

Walking down Buzz's street, you can hear the thumping and guitar sounds of Taxadurmee coming out of his garage. I talked Brianna into waiting until the song was over before going in.

Everyone said hi to us, then Buzz wanted to play that same song again. I'm not sure if he wanted to work on it some more or just do it again so we could hear it. Doug, who plays the drums, looked like he didn't want to play it again, but he didn't say anything. I think it's Buzz's band more than Doug's, and it's definitely Buzz's garage.

You could tell they were all a little nervous about playing for us, and I don't mean because they think Dave Motts can help them. It's just different doing something for an audience.

Like my podcasts. I can work for ten hours on

a one-minute podcast. I'll put it together and I'll watch it over and over and over again and keep making little changes until I think it's perfect.

Then I show it to someone. It doesn't even matter who. Because as soon as someone else is there, you see it the way they're seeing it. Even before they tell you what they think, you know. The middle part is boring. You have to fix it.

I like this song. So does Brianna, from the look on her face. Buzz is singing it right to her. Well, we're all in the garage together, and the band is facing us, and there are only two of us in the audience. But trust me, he's singing to her.

I don't know what this song is about, but I think sometimes that doesn't matter so much with songs. I've downloaded some songs and listened to them like a hundred times, and even though I know every word, I still don't know what they're supposed to be about. I just like them.

My songs, the ones on my podcast I mean, are the opposite of this. You always know exactly what they're about. This one's about dogs. This one's about donuts. This one's about my cousin's bar mitzvah. That's what's so great about music. You can like Buzz's songs and you can like my songs, and you can also like the songs your parents liked when they were teenagers. You don't have to choose. Whatever you like, you just like.

As much as I like this new song, I was relieved when it was over, because with Buzz singing it right to Brianna, it was a little embarrassing standing there. I didn't know where to look. I didn't want to look at him and I didn't want to look at her. I definitely didn't want to look at Doug playing the drums. So that left Slade and Remy.

Slade plays guitar, and when he plays, he looks like someone trying to look like a guy in a band playing guitar. He keeps jumping around and making these faces that don't go with the song. It's like he's imagining being in a different band, *his* band, where people are watching *him*, not Buzz. It's too weird.

I ended up watching Remy, who plays the bass guitar. Remy just stands still and plays. You can tell he's listening to Buzz and following along, and he looks like he's happy to be here.

When the song ended, they took a break. At Buzz's house, in the room near the garage, they have a freezer with every possible snack you could ever want. There's a microwave there too, in case the snack you choose is pizza or a taco.

Brianna asked Buzz for a tour of the house, and they disappeared. Whatever adult was in the house, we never saw them. I was eating ice cream when Doug walked over.

"We sound good, right?"

"You do. I like the new song."

"Call Dave Motts and we'll play it for him over the phone."

"No. I can't just call him at night."

"Why not? He's in California, right?"

Uh-oh. I never actually decided where Dave Motts lives. Or Dan Welch.

"I don't even *know* where he lives. I don't even have his phone number."

"Yes you do. He's your agent, right?"

"Dave Motts is not my agent." (Technically true.)

"Wait a minute, you little—"

Then Buzz and Brianna walked back in. She looks happy.

"Doug . . . I'll do what I can. I promise."

I better figure something out soon.

chapter 9

I think I should go visit my grandmother. Those are words I never actually said before in my whole life. I'm not saying I don't like my grandmother. I do. Both of my grandmothers. I love them. But that doesn't mean I want to spend a lot of time with them. Usually about an hour is good.

The whole idea for *A Week with Your Grandparents* came because my parents were thinking about having a second honeymoon. The first one was a disaster. Well, that's what I heard. I wasn't born yet. When they told me they suddenly wanted a second one, they said I could stay with my grandmother. I said no.

I have two grandmothers. My mom's mom, who

we call Mary Lou, lives in a senior living place. We see her every year, but I've only seen where she lives once. She has a bedroom, a bathroom, and a fridge, but no kitchen. She eats all her meals in a dining room at big tables with other old people. I might want to do my podcast there, but I couldn't actually stay with Mary Lou.

Not that she'd want me to. Mary Lou had six children (including my mom), and after all that, she had enough of kids. She likes to see her grandchildren, but only a little. *Less* than an hour, actually. At first I thought it was just me, but my cousins say the same thing. They all live near Mary Lou. My mom was the only one in her family who moved to another state. "It's better this way, Sean. We can have a nice little visit, then we can leave."

My other grandmother is the one I might visit. She's my dad's mother, and she lives in another state too. The state of Florida. We see her a little more often. She only had two kids, so even though she complains about us sometimes, she actually likes being with her grandchildren. Sometimes we

visit her and sometimes she visits us. When I talk
to her, I call her Grandma, but when I talk about
her, I call her by the name she made up for her
email address. It's ThornyRosen@ _____.com,
but I just say Thorny.

The grandmother in *A Week with Your
Grandparents* is like Thorny in certain ways. She
has opinions about everything, which she tells
you even if you don't ask her. Her main opinion
is that everything is getting worse. "It's all falling
apart. It's terrible."

Thorny and my dad argue all the time, but she
and I have fun together. I think she's annoying
sometimes, and she thinks I'm annoying
sometimes, but in a funny way. We argue, but we
don't get mad, like my dad sometimes does. He
keeps thinking he can change her mind.

I never knew Thorny's husband, my dad's dad.
He died before I was born. No one ever talked
about Grandpa, but a few months ago my dad told
me what happened. It was pretty bad. He actually
went to prison. He had a business that stole money
from people. I can't believe someone in my family

did that. The rest of us are so not criminals.

I hope. I'm a little worried that making up a manager might be a crime. But what would the crime be? Signing a made-up name to an email I actually wrote? Probably not.

Anyway, I want to visit Thorny for two reasons. I want to ask her some questions. What was Grandpa like? Did he act like a criminal? Was he sorry for what he did? Did you know he was stealing? How did you find out?

I could ask my dad. Or even my mom, because she knew him too. But Grandma knew him better. She married him. I don't know if she'll tell me, but maybe she will after we're together for a little while.

The second reason I want to visit her is research for my screenplay. I mostly understand the kids in my movie. Chris is a little older than me, and Chloe's a little younger. They're the kind of kids I know. But the grandparents . . . I usually know what they would do and what they would say. But I don't always know why.

Here's an example. In the movie, we find out that Grandpa invented the virtual reality time machine a long time ago. He and Grandma tried it out and it actually works, but Grandma would never let him sell it, or even show it to anyone. I know she thinks it would be bad for the world, but I don't know why.

That's something Thorny might do. She always complains about new things, but a lot of the time, I think she's wrong. New things are cool. Think about it. I can record a podcast right here in my town. Then, sitting in my room, I can edit it and put it on the internet. A second later, someone I don't even know, like Collectibles Dan Welch, can sit in his house (wherever that is) and watch that exact podcast.

Collectibles still hasn't forwarded that email about me to Dan Welch. It's only been a day and six hours, but it only takes a few seconds to forward an email. And Collectibles seems like he's always online. Maybe he went somewhere to buy a doll or an autograph or something.

I check Dan Welch's email account all the time, but I never check my own. Even though I don't use email very much, my grandmothers do. Maybe there's something from Thorny that's been sitting there for a really long time. If I'm visiting her soon, I don't want it to start out with her being mad at me.

There's something in my inbox, but it's not from Thorny. It's from Martin Manager (not his real name). Martin manages some famous people in show business, and before I got Dan Welch, I tried to get Martin to manage me. He wouldn't because he doesn't believe in managing kids, but he's nice. He gave me advice once. I didn't think I'd ever hear from him again.

To: Sean Rosen
From: Martin Manager

Dear Sean,

From the first time you wrote to me, I had a feeling I'd be hearing more about you, and it happened today. I was having lunch at the commissary at _____ (the studio Hank Hollywood is Chairman of), and a couple of high-level assistants were talking about you. It was along the lines of "Have you heard of this kid Sean Rosen?" and "Do you know what his idea is?"

You're the talk of Hollywood. I don't know how you do it, Sean, but you *do* write a good letter, and maybe you've been writing a lot of them lately. Or maybe just a strategic few.

One of the women at lunch was someone I don't know, but the other one, the one asking the questions, works for the big guy there—Hank Hollywood (he used his real name). Out here, Hank is the shark that scares all the other sharks.

Did you end up selling your idea to Stefanie President? Or have you somehow managed to start a bidding war? See, Sean? You don't need a manager. (He doesn't know about Dan Welch.)

Good luck. Be careful.

Best,
Martin

chapter 10

I like Saturday mornings. First of all, there's no school. I don't hate school, but I don't love school. My main problem with it is that it's all day long, and there are a lot of other things I'd rather be doing. The parts of school that I like only take up a few hours, but then you're stuck there for the rest of the day.

So Saturday morning you wake up and you remember it's not a school day. I love that feeling. I also like Saturday because it isn't Sunday. So you're not thinking about how it's all going to start again tomorrow.

I didn't feel like getting out of bed yet, so I ran

over and got my laptop and got back under the covers.

Brianna changed her Facebook status to "In a Relationship." That was fast. I wonder if Buzz knows. He isn't on Facebook.

I checked Dan Welch's inbox. Collectibles still hasn't forwarded that email. Why not? What's in that email?? Who is it from???

Hank Hollywood and his assistant have Dan's email address, but for some reason, they're not writing back. They're just asking other people about me. Why? It's weird. Why can't we just have a Skype meeting?

It would be so easy. I'll tell him the idea, he'll love it, and we can start working on it together. If we don't get started soon, someone else is going to think of it.

I Googled Hank Hollywood again. Oh my God. You know how much money he makes? Fifty million dollars a year. That's like a million dollars a week. I get ten dollars a week.

Maybe Hank Hollywood thinks he doesn't need

my idea. But he *does*. Trust me, they'll give him a big raise.

Okay, I have to get up. I'm glad Ethan is coming over. I could tell him about all this, and I probably will someday. But not today. Today we're working on the podcast.

Ethan moved to our town this year, a few months after school started. He's very quiet, but he's also the only one who gets every funny thing I ever say or do. He's funny too, but you'd never know it. His voice never changes, no matter what he's saying. His face doesn't either. So when he says something funny, it takes you a second to get it, but then it's even funnier because he said it that way. I keep trying to get him to talk on the podcast, but so far he won't.

This is the third Saturday of working with Ethan on the podcast. I was used to doing it by myself, but it's actually more fun this way. I'm not the world's biggest kid, but *he* might be (he's gigantic—really tall, really big, not fat, just extra large), so we probably look funny when we walk into a place together. He usually stands off to the side while I do the interviews, but I know he's there if I need anything. And he started taking some of the pictures. He's good at it. When you look at the podcast, you probably can't tell who took which pictures.

Ethan comes over around ten, and we have breakfast with whoever's home. The first week it was just my dad. My dad makes really good breakfasts. They always include bacon. The second week my dad was out on a job, but my mom had the day off. She makes good breakfasts too. She's more of a fruit-and-yogurt person. Today they're both here.

DAD:	(to Ethan) **You like bacon, right?**
ETHAN:	**Yeah.**
DAD:	**Do you like rugelach?**
ETHAN:	**Do I like *what*?**
ME:	**Some people pronounce it roo-gela.**
MOM:	(to me) **That's not it,**

	honey. (then to Ethan, holding one up) **This.** It's like a Jewish cookie. I never heard of it either. I mean, before I was a Rosen.
DAD:	Her family is about as un-Rosen as they get.
MOM:	Ethan, what's *your* family like?
DAD:	Here she goes.
ME:	Ethan, you have the right to remain silent.
DAD:	Seriously. You don't have to answer her questions. You won't hurt her feelings.
MOM:	These two already took care of *that*. (to Dad and me) I refuse to apologize for being interested in people. (then to Ethan) So . . . what's your family like?
ETHAN:	Small. Then it got even smaller.

Everyone was quiet for a few seconds.

ETHAN: **My brother died.**
ME: **He did?**

I don't know why I said that. It just came out.

ETHAN: Yeah.
DAD: Recently?
ETHAN: Last summer.

My digital voice recorder was right there in the kitchen, sitting on the counter. Sometimes I just leave it on. I have a big memory card, and I like recording things, even just breakfast with my family. I wasn't expecting anything like this to happen.

I looked over at the recorder. You can see that the red light is on. I want to go over and turn it off, but I don't want anyone to know it was on in the first place. I shouldn't be recording this. I have to stop looking at it. I don't know if I should be looking at Ethan right now, but I do.

ME: That's really sad.

Ethan nodded. He didn't say anything. But he wasn't looking down like he does when he doesn't want to talk.

DAD: You're gonna love bacon and
           rugelach.

Ethan laughed.

MOM: (to Ethan) As you heard, my
           family thinks I ask too
           many questions, but I want
           you to know . . . I'm not
           nosy. I'm interested.
ETHAN: Go ahead. It's okay.
MOM: Really?
ETHAN: Yeah.
MOM: What happened?
ETHAN: A car hit him.
DAD: Hit and run?
ETHAN: No. A friend of his. He was

> drunk. The friend, I mean.
> Not my brother.

MOM: Oh, Ethan.

My mom actually started to cry.

Ethan got up and pointed to the rugelach.

ETHAN: *What* did you say this is
called?

Today we're working on a library podcast. The library is pretty close to my house. After breakfast, Ethan and I walked there. On the way, I usually talk about who we're going to interview and what I want pictures of, but today I was quiet. I couldn't stop thinking about Ethan's brother. I guess he could tell.

"You can ask me questions if you want."

"Are you sure?"

"Yeah."

What was his name?"

"Dwight. Everyone called him Skip."

"What was he like?"

"The opposite of me."

"What do you mean?"

"Great athlete. Everyone liked him."

"Including you?"

"He didn't bother much with me."

We walked some more.

"Are you glad you moved?"

"Yeah. I got tired of getting sad looks from everyone."

"What about your parents?"

"What about them?"

"Are they like . . . I don't know. . . . How are they?"

"You were in my house."

Once when we were riding bikes I had to use the bathroom, and we stopped at Ethan's house. It was weird. Very dark, and it looked like they never really moved in. When we got there, his mom didn't say hi. It looked like she actually hid.

I didn't know what else to say, so I started talking about the podcast.

chapter 11

I grew up going to this library. They know me here. I came in the other day to ask if it was okay to do my podcast there. They didn't exactly know what I was talking about, but they said yes.

This man named Carl is sitting at a table. He's always at the library. Like every single time I've been there. I don't know anything about him. I can't decide if I should interview him. I want to find out about him, but I'm not sure I want to be the one who finds it out.

If I interview him, will he talk to me every time I come to the library? That happened from some of the other podcasts. They were always nice to me at the barber shop, but now when I go to get my hair cut, they all come over. And the girl who works at the donut place sort of smiles at me when I come in now. She never did that before.

"Ethan, what do you think?"

"Go ahead. Talk to him."

So I did. I walked up to him. I waited until he stopped writing, which took a while. A minute and twelve seconds, actually. That's a long time to stand next to someone.

"Hi, Carl."

He looked at me, but he didn't say anything.

"We don't really know each other, but we both use this library. My name is Sean."

He still didn't say anything.

"This thing I'm holding is a digital voice recorder. I'm actually recording right now. I'm interviewing people."

"About what?"

"The library."

"What about it?"

"What do you like the best about it?"

"When it's quiet."

Ethan, who was standing on the side, almost started laughing.

I said, "I like that part, too. And I'm gonna stop talking soon, I promise. Do you remember the first time you went to a library?"

"The first time? I was a little kid. Younger than you. What are you? Around ten?"

Ethan turned away from us because this time he actually *did* start laughing.

"I'm thirteen."

"Well, I must have been six. Or eight. My mother took me to some art class. You know, drawing. I hate drawing. I can't draw. So one week we'd have to draw a horse, and another week it was a pear. It didn't matter what it was. My horse looked exactly like my pear. I gave up trying. I'd scribble something on my paper, then get up and hide in the shelves."

"The teacher let you do that?"

"She didn't even notice. She was too busy with the kids who could draw. I would randomly pick books off the shelf and read until my mother came and got me. Nonfiction."

"Even when you were six? Or eight?"

"Nonfiction. I don't like stories."

"How do you decide what to read?"

"Subject matter."

"Do you look inside the book?"

"That's where the words are."

"No. I mean when you're deciding."

"Oh. No. Maybe the introduction."

"What are you reading today?"

"Do I have to tell you?"

"Do you *have* to? No. I mean, I want to know. But it's up to you."

"*Thermal Propulsion Theory.*"

"How is it?"

"I don't know. I haven't finished it yet."

"Do you ever take books out of the library?"

"No. I read them here."

"Well, thanks for talking to me. We'll try to be quiet."

"Good."

I interviewed six or seven other people, some kids, some grown-ups, and a few of the people who work there. Ethan took a lot of good pictures. Carl was still there when we left. I think it's going to be an interesting podcast when I get around to editing it, and writing and recording the song. I have no idea what the song will be, but I'm not worried. I don't really run out of ideas. They're not all good, but I keep having them.

Leaving the library, Ethan lives in one direction and I live in the other. When we said good-bye, I thought about saying something about his brother. Dwight. Or Skip. But then I thought maybe we talked about him enough today. And Ethan seemed like he was in a good mood. I didn't want to change it. I wasn't sure I could talk about his brother without having a sad look.

I got home and went right to my room to check Dan Welch's email. Nothing from Collectibles yet. I'm going crazy. It's been more than two days!

Dan Welch would probably tell me to calm down, but he wants to know too. I thought for a

minute about whether Dan Welch ever works on
the weekend. I think he sometimes does.

To: Dan Welch
From: Dan Welch Management

Dear Dan,

Thanks for the offer, but I checked with my wife, and
she doesn't want me to buy that Farrah Fawcett poster.

I'm sure you're busy, but I hope you can forward
that email about Sean Rosen. I'm curious, and
unfortunately, I made the mistake of mentioning it to
Sean. You know what thirteen-year-old boys are like.
You used to be one.

So do me a big favor and send that email as soon as
you can.

Best,
Dan

chapter 12

On the way home from school today I saw Mrs. Dahlin, who lives near us. She and her husband are really nice, and best of all, they're the people who have Baxter. I asked Mrs. Dahlin if I could walk him later, and she said yes.

I've played with Baxter a lot, and I've played with a lot of other dogs, too. But I never actually took any of them for a walk. I've *been* with people and their dogs on a walk. I know what happens. But I've never been in charge of it.

If I tell my mom I'm going to walk Baxter she'll be glad, because she thinks I only *think* I want a dog, and if I see how much work it is, I'll get over it. I actually don't think I will.

But I *am* a little nervous. What if Baxter doesn't want to go with me? What if he runs away? What if he gets into a fight with another dog?

I rang the doorbell, and Baxter started barking. I'm not worried anymore. I know Baxter, and Baxter knows me. We're friends. Who wouldn't want to go for a walk with a friend?

In my dog podcast (www.SeanRosen.com/dogs), I ask people if their dogs want to get walked more often than they *do* get walked. Almost everyone says yes. But I didn't ask the dogs.

Do people really know what their dogs think, or do they just *think* they do? I bet they're wrong sometimes. Like my parents. With me, I mean.

Last week my mom came home from the store and said she got me my favorite cookies. I think she wanted me to help unpack the bags. When I finally got to the cookies, I couldn't believe it.

"You think *these* are my favorites?"

"They're not?"

"No."

"They *were*."

"For like a week. Like four or five years ago."

"And now you hate them?"

"They're okay. They're definitely not my favorites."

"Is this your creative way of saying thank you?"

I wasn't sure I should thank her. She doesn't know my favorites. Her guess was way off. She got me excited for nothing. And I unpacked three bags of groceries before I figured it out.

"Thank you, Mom."

"You're welcome. I'll try to stay up-to-date on your preferences."

"Okay."

"Shall I return these cookies?"

"You don't have to."

"I can."

"No."

"Are you sure?"

"I want one now."

———————

Mrs. Dahlin opened the door, and Baxter jumped on me to say hello. Mrs. Dahlin said, "Hi, Sean. As you can see, Baxter is very excited about your walk."

"Oh, good. I am too."

"I usually take him out by now, but since I knew you were going to, I didn't."

I was sort of hoping Mrs. Dahlin already took Baxter out to do his business, so he and I could just have a nice relaxing walk. Oh, well. "Is there anything I should know?"

"If you can, have him poop in the street. You know, instead of on someone's lawn."

"How do I get him to do that?"

"Oh . . . you know . . . just stay in the street. Not the *middle* of the street, of course. He'll want to get on the grass. He can poop on the grass in the park, but I don't think he's gonna make it till you get there. Did you bring a bag?"

"A bag?"

"For the poop."

"Oh. Actually I didn't."

"Don't worry. Here you go. Take three, just in case."

"Three?"

"He hardly ever poops three times, but you don't want to run out of bags."

"No, I don't. This might be a really stupid question, but how do you . . . you know . . . get it into the bag?"

"Easy-peasy. You put your hand in the bag, like this, and just pick up the poop, like the bag is a glove. Then you turn the bag inside out. You never have to touch the poop. Unless there's a hole in the bag."

I started looking at the plastic bags.

"Don't worry, Sean. I checked these. Then you just drop it in the garbage."

"*Any* garbage?"

"Maybe wait until you get to the park. People are funny about dog poop in their trash bins, even if it's bagged. Just bring it to the park. It'll keep your hands warm. Okay, you two should get going. Baxter's more than ready. Shall I put his leash on?"

"No. *I* will." If I'm going to do this, I might as well really do it.

It was a little hard to get the leash on because Baxter was jumping around, and I had all these plastic bags. I was going to ask for a fourth bag just in case, but once the leash was on, Baxter dragged me out the door.

Baxter was pulling me a little faster than I wanted to go. Even though I'm bigger than him, he decides. I kept us in the street, which wasn't very easy. Just like Mrs. Dahlin said, Baxter kept pulling me toward people's lawns.

We didn't get very far when Baxter stopped, and started pooping. I wasn't sure if I should watch or not. Do dogs like to have privacy? Just to be safe, I looked the other way. Then I felt a tug on the leash. I didn't know how I would know when he was finished, but it was easy to tell. He just walked away from it. I wish *I* could, too.

"Wait a sec, Baxter." I took one of the plastic bags out of my pocket, and I looked at the poop in the street. I thought about leaving it there, and I even thought about whether poop has DNA in it, so it could be traced back to Baxter, but only for a few seconds. If I'm ever going to have a dog, I have to be able to do this.

I wanted to hold my nose, but I had the plastic bag in one hand and Baxter's leash in the other.

So I just did it the way Mrs. Dahlin showed me. It works.

It ended up being a very relaxing walk. I threw away the bag of poop when we got to the park. It didn't keep my hand warm. Mrs. Dahlin probably holds the bag a different way.

ollectibles Dan Welch finally wrote back to
Dan Welch. I thought he was just going to forward
that email about me, but he didn't.

To: Dan Welch Management
From: Dan Welch

Hey Dan,

I was surprised to get your e-mail. Nothing
from you for months, then twice in 1 week!

Too bad your wife wont let you have Farrah.
You could always get it and put it somewhere

she never goes. If shes like my ex, that would be the laundry room. If you ask her about me, yule get another story so please dont.

So. That email. Heres what they said.

He copied and pasted it, but left out who it's from.

Dear Dan Welch,

I'm writing about Sean Rosen. I was at Sean's pitch meeting for the movie. I'm at a different studio now, and I'd like to talk to you about it. Before I go any further, can you let me know you're the right Dan Welch?

Best,

Very interesting! You know I like Sean's podcasts, but I had no clue your in the movie biz. Cool! Nice managing, Dan Welch.

Tell me about this movie. Maybe I can help. I'm not exagurating when I tell you that at least 5 sepurate people have said to me, "DW, your life should be a movie." Your boy Sean couldn't see it, tho. RAted R, to say the least.

So tell me what you want me to tell this person and I'll pass it along. Glad to help.

Later,
Dan

Why couldn't he just forward the email? It would have been so easy. For him and for us. Now we have to figure out who it's from.

There were four other people at that meeting besides Stefanie V. President and me: Stefanie's assistant, Brad, and her three Directors of Development, Ashley, Devin, and Eva. I don't know any of their last names.

It can't be Brad, because he already has Dan Welch's email address. He wrote to us a few times.

But what if Brad got a new job? Then he might not have Dan Welch's email anymore. They probably don't let you keep your computer when you leave.

Actually, I don't think he left. Brad and Stefanie seem like they belong together. Plus, I spoke to Brad and also got some emails from him. This doesn't sound like Brad.

That leaves Ashley, Devin, or Eva. I have no idea which of them it could be. I wonder how I can figure it out. *The Hollywood Reporter* has a page called "Hitched, Hatched, Hired," where they tell you who in Hollywood got married, who had a baby, and who got a new job. I looked at the last five issues (I save them all), but it looks like they don't ever write about Directors of Development on that page. You have to be higher up.

I Googled each of their first names, plus Director of Development, plus the name of Stefanie's studio, but I couldn't find anything.

Then I called the studio's main number, to see if I could find out who still works there. Here's how *that* went.

ME: **Can you connect me with a Director of Development named Eva?** (CLICK)

I recorded that Skype meeting with Stefanie and the rest of them on my digital voice recorder, so I listened to it again. I thought maybe I could get some kind of clue about whether it was Ashley, Devin, or Eva who was going to quit soon and go to work at another studio. But those three hardly said anything during the meeting, so I can't really tell.

While I had my digital voice recorder out, I deleted the recording that I made of Ethan and my parents in our kitchen last Saturday. I never would have been recording if I knew he was going to tell us about his brother. I was a little tempted to listen to it once before I deleted it, but it didn't feel right. Anyway, I'm not going to forget that conversation.

Okay. What do we do about this mystery email?

I think we have two choices. Dan Welch can reply, and then send it to Collectibles Dan

Welch to pass it along to whichever Director of Development it is.

That could get annoying. Actually, it already is annoying.

The other choice is to just write to Stefanie and tell her we got an email from one of her ex-Directors of Development. I wonder if that would be okay. Is it a secret that someone who used to work there is interested in my movie? He or she didn't say, "Don't tell Stefanie." At least I *think* they didn't. I never saw the whole email.

All of this made me think about something Martin Manager asked me in his email.

Did you end up selling your idea to Stefanie President? Or have you somehow managed to start a bidding war?

I don't exactly know what he means by a bidding war. I just looked it up. Wikipedia says it's something about the card game War, but I know Martin wasn't talking about a card game. Looking at other things that came up in Google, I think a bidding war is when more than one person wants something you have. Like for example, a movie idea. Let's say it's called *A Week with Your Grandparents*.

Stefanie's studio offered us 10,000 dollars for the idea (plus the characters and the sequels and the theme park ride and anything else they might ever want). Then if Ashley, Devin, or Eva's new studio *also* wanted it, they might offer us a bid of 15,000 dollars. Then Dan Welch could say to Stefanie, "We have an offer from another studio for 15,000 dollars. If you want it, you have to raise your bid."

And it wouldn't even matter which ex-Director of Development and which studio it was. The important thing is that someone else wants it, and if *you* want it, you have to bid more to get it. Like when Stefanie offered to "sweeten the pot" after she got the call from Hank Hollywood about me.

Let the war begin!

To: Stefanie V. President
From: Dan Welch Management

Dear Stefanie,

I apologize for not getting back to you after your nice letter. Things have gotten very busy around here.

I'm glad to hear you're back at work and that Marisa is doing well. My wife encourages you to be patient. It gets easier.

I told Sean you sent him a hug, and he sends you one too. It's hard to believe the two of you never met in person. He's very fond of you and said to tell you he's having a great time writing *A Week with Your Grandparents*. Maybe you're right that it's hard to write a screenplay (I've never tried), but you'd never know it talking to Sean. He thinks it's coming out great.

Thanks for the warning about Hank Hollywood. As someone once told me, "He's the shark who scares the other sharks."

We just heard from someone else you used to work with who wants to talk to us about *A Week with Your Grandparents*. I thought you'd want to know.

Yes, I do know the kinds of movies you make, and I promise to think about other clients you might want to meet. Meanwhile, I told Sean that you want to hear his other ideas. Be careful. He's got a lot of them.

Best,
Dan

chapter 14

Today was a terrible day at school. And it got terrible in ways I wasn't even expecting.

I was in such a good mood when I got to English. It's my favorite class, and I was happy to see Miss Meglis, my favorite teacher.

"Okay, new and soon-to-be teenagers"—she calls us something different every day—"we all know what today is. The long-awaited, much-anticipated due date for your short stories. I'll collect them now."

My heart stopped beating. I totally forgot. When we got the email from Collectibles I got so excited about the bidding war that I completely forgot about school.

I almost always do my homework. Even for classes I don't like. How did this happen?

My mom usually asks me at dinner if I have homework, but she worked the evening shift at the hospital last night. My dad never asks me. I swear, I'm not blaming them, but that's part of what happened. But the main part was me thinking about my movie and not about school.

It was awful sitting there watching everyone else turn in their stories. It would have been so easy for me to write mine. In fact, I *did* write mine, but only in my head. I'm lucky that writing is easy for me, so it was really stupid not to do it.

"I don't have mine. I'm sorry. I'll have it tomorrow."

Miss Meglis just stood there. It took her a minute to believe it. I sounded like some other kid.

"I'm disappointed in you, Sean. You'll lose points." She didn't whisper this. It was loud enough for everyone to hear.

I don't want to lose points, but it's worse having my favorite teacher disappointed in me. It's depressing. I didn't raise my hand during the whole class, which is unusual for me. I sometimes stay for a minute at the end to talk to Miss Meglis, but I didn't today. It would feel like I was trying to get her to not take off points and to tell me I could have an extra day. But she knows and I know that I didn't really need an extra day.

Then, walking to my next class, I hear, "Thanks for telling me about Dave Motts."

It's Brianna. Buzz must have told her.

"I thought we were friends, Sean."

"We are."

"Friends don't keep secrets from friends."

Sometimes they do.

Then she said, "You know someone in the music business and you didn't *tell* me?"

"Well, I . . ."

"'Well, I . . .'" She was imitating me. "I looked for him online last night and I couldn't find him."

"Well . . ."

"M-O-T-T-S, right?"

"Right. Like the applesauce. You know, managers don't really have websites."

"I also asked my dad to ask his friend in the music business."

"You know someone in the music business and you didn't—"

"Don't even *try* it, Sean. Anyway, he never even heard of Dave Motts."

"The music business is huge. Everyone doesn't know everyone. Maybe your dad's friend can help Taxadurmee."

"Leave him out of it. *You're* the one who said you could help. Whoever this Dave Motts is, why is he taking so long to listen to two songs?"

"I don't know, Brianna. He's probably very busy."

"With what? Your *movie*? *What* movie? Now you have a *movie*? Did you just make all this up to impress Buzz?"

Thank goodness the bell rang. What is happening? Everyone who used to like me is suddenly mad at me. I just want to go somewhere and hide.

I came home after school, grabbed my laptop,

and sat down at the dining-room table. That's where I sit when I have to do serious work. I didn't let myself have a snack. I didn't look at email, mine or Dan Welch's. I closed out of the internet so I wouldn't even be tempted.

I just sat there and wrote my short story. My dad came home. He saw me at the dining-room table concentrating really hard and typing really fast, so he didn't even say hello. I didn't either. I wanted to stay inside the story.

It's about a quiet man who's in the library every day, reading books and taking notes. No one knows anything about him, except his name. Clyde.

One day Clyde doesn't come to the library. He doesn't come the next day either. On the third day, the librarians start to get worried about him.

Clyde is not a friendly guy. He never even says hello to the librarians, who he sees every day. Still, they're used to him being there, sitting at the same table, concentrating really hard on whatever book he's reading and taking pages and pages of notes on yellow paper.

He brings his own pencil sharpener, and

sometimes when he leaves at the end of the day, they find his pencil sharpenings on the table. He usually stays until the library closes, and he keeps working until the end, so he doesn't have time to clean up.

On the fourth day that Clyde doesn't come to the library, Becky, one of the librarians, decides to try to find out why. She doesn't tell the other librarians, but she's really worried about Clyde.

She doesn't even know if he has a library card, because he never takes out books. When she's alone at the front desk, she secretly does a search of the thousands of people with library cards. There's only one person named Clyde. It's probably him.

There's no phone number, but there's an address. If you want a library card, you have to bring in something with your address on it. Maybe when he first started coming, Clyde thought he would want to take out books.

After work, even though she knows she shouldn't, Becky goes to that address to see if it's the right Clyde, and to see if he's okay. She gets to a small house. There's a light on. She's a little nervous, but she rings the doorbell. She doesn't hear any sound, and no one comes to the door. She rings it again. And again.

She thinks maybe the doorbell is broken, so she knocks on the door. The door just opens. It wasn't completely closed. She doesn't know what to do.

"Clyde?"

No one answers.

"Clyde, are you in there?"

No one answers.

"Clyde, it's Becky from the library."

There's no sound.

"Oh. You probably don't know our names. I'm the one you ask to watch your stuff when you go to the bathroom."

She still doesn't hear anything. She decides to go in.

No one's there. There are piles of things everywhere. You can't tell from looking at the house if someone robbed it, or if someone just lives like this.

Becky knows she should just stop now and leave, but she can't. She's always been curious about Clyde, and sometimes, when he goes to the bathroom, she sneaks a look at what he's writing on that yellow paper he uses. It's always a lot of numbers and symbols, and words she doesn't know, even though she's very smart.

She can see through the kitchen that the back door is open too. She walks through the kitchen, which isn't as bad as she thought it would be, and goes into the backyard.

It's not that big, but there's a tall fence around it. She can tell that Clyde wants privacy, and that makes her think she should leave. Just then, she notices a big circle on the ground where the grass looks burned.

She decides to leave. She goes back inside. She isn't sure if she should touch anything, including the back door, but she feels funny leaving it open. She does, though, and then walks back through the house. On her way to the front door, she sees something she didn't see before.

It's a library book. Becky knows that Clyde never checks out books, so she's surprised to see one. She goes over and looks closely, and sure enough, it's from her library. Clyde must have stolen it. Becky is surprised, because she never thought of Clyde as a thief.

The name of the book is *Thermal Propulsion Theory*. It's a complicated science book, but looking at it, Becky can see that it's about launching and flying a spacecraft, using solar power. She sees that someone wrote notes in pencil inside the book. It looks like Clyde's handwriting.

Did Clyde build a rocket? Did he launch himself into space? Becky looks around and doesn't see a note anywhere. She decides she really has to leave. She didn't touch anything, except for the library book. Part of her wants to take the book back to the library, but she decides to leave it where it is. She moves the front door with her leg so it looks closed, even though it's really not, just like when she got there.

Becky goes home and searches the internet to see if any rockets crashed anywhere in the world this week. She doesn't find anything.

Clyde never comes back to the library. When the other librarians talk about Clyde and where he might be, Becky doesn't say anything. Part of it is that she knows she shouldn't have gone into his house. The other part is that she knows Clyde didn't want anyone to know what he was doing.

But now, at night, whenever Becky looks up at the stars, she says, "Hi, Clyde. Hope you're okay."

chapter 15

kept writing until I finished. Then I printed it out, read it over, made some changes, then printed it out again. It's dark outside. Hours went by, and I didn't even notice. My dad heard me get up and yelled from the family room, "Pizza okay?" That means my mom is working a double shift.

"Okay."

"When?"

"Forty-five minutes?"

"Okay."

I read my story out loud again. Quietly, so my dad wouldn't think I was still talking to him. That's the way I proofread, and you also get to hear how it's going to sound to whoever else is going to read it.

I'm glad I did, because I ended up changing about ten things. Which meant I had to print it again. It uses up a lot of paper and ink to do it this way, but I think it's worth it (even though it's not *me* paying for the paper and ink). If it's going to be late, I want it to be good. With writing, I always want it to be good.

My dad and I sometimes have pizza on trays in front of the TV, but I told him I want to eat in the kitchen tonight. I have more work to do, and I don't want to get interested in a TV show. I might be tempted to keep watching it.

"Why so serious, Seany?"

"Oh, I don't know."

"You know. But if you don't want to tell me, don't."

Do I want to tell him?

"Well . . . I forgot to do an English assignment."

"And . . . ?"

"Now it's done."

"Okay. What else?"

He's starting to sound like my mom. She's the detective in the family. I guess it's rubbing off on him.

"Oh . . . I told some friends I'd help them with something."

"And now you don't want to?"

"No. I want to. I just don't know if I can. I mean if I'm actually able to. You know, actually *help* them."

"Did you try?"

"Not yet."

"What are you waiting for?"

I had to think about that.

"I've been busy. But that's not it. I guess I'm afraid I'll find out I really *can't* help them."

"And you don't want to let them down?"

"I don't. But it's more than that."

"Yeah?"

"I don't know . . . I liked the feeling. You know, of being someone who can do things for people. Of having them think I'm like . . . important or something."

"Yeah. I know what you mean. Be careful with that, Seany. That's part of what got my father in trouble."

Oh, no. I *am* like Grandpa.

"What do you mean?"

"He made the people whose money he stole feel like they were lucky to be in business with him. That was part of the turn-on for him. Do you know what I mean?"

"Sort of."

"He liked feeling important. He liked the feeling that people were chasing after him. His customers, I mean. Not the law."

I got a sick feeling. It sounds exactly like me with the bidding war.

"Seany . . . maybe you don't want me to talk about Grandpa."

"No, no. I do. Really. I want to know about him. I just don't want to *be* like him."

"I don't think you are."

"I hope not. I do like feeling important sometimes."

"Everyone does. But the best way to be

important to your friends is to be a good friend."

I thought about that.

"You're right." I got up.

"All done?"

"Yeah. Is that okay? I gotta go see if I can actually help these friends."

"Go."

"Thanks, Dad."

I started to run out of the kitchen. Then I stopped.

"You don't know anyone in the music business, do you?"

He thought for a few seconds.

"Bar mitzvah deejay?"

"Thanks anyway."

Okay, let's figure this out. What can I actually do for Taxadurmee? What can Dave Motts do?

I can put their music on my website. But what good would *that* do? I like my podcasts and my songs, but Buzz's songs are very, very different. I actually don't think that SeanRosen.com is the right place for Taxadurmee.

I guess I can think about who else in music reminds me of Taxadurmee, and then I can look up those bands and try to find the companies they work with. Then Dave Motts can send the MP3 to those companies, and maybe they'll like Taxadurmee and want to buy their songs.

That sounds like a lot of work. I still have my own career. Plus I have to go to school. And turn in English papers on time.

Why did I tell them I could help? Oh. I remember. Doug made me. I'm supposed to get my manager, Dave Motts, to be *their* manager, too.

All I really promised them was that I would get Dave Motts to listen to their songs. *That* I can actually do. I know Dave Motts. I *am* Dave Motts. Okay, so Dave Motts will listen to their songs. He'll *like* them too. I know he will. But then what?

I remember the first time I read something nice Dan Welch wrote about me. It made me feel good. Not good. Great.

I know. I wrote it myself. You think I'm crazy. You're right. But still. It gave me confidence. So here we go.

To: Sean Rosen

From: Dave Motts

Dear Sean,

First I have to apologize for the long delay getting back to you. I didn't want to tell you until I was absolutely sure about this, but I am both glad and sad to tell you that I am retiring from being a manager.

Our kids are grown, and my wife has always wanted to live in South America, so we are moving to Paraguay. I will miss the entertainment business, but I'm looking forward to this adventure. I'm sorry we never got to work together. You have a lot of energy and some good ideas. Keep trying.

I listened to the MP3 you sent me. You're right. Taxadurmee has a unique sound. I like them and so do my kids. I would pass along the MP3 to someone, but the people I know are in film and television, not music.

Please tell the band I think they're on the right track. They should definitely keep writing songs, and play for audiences whenever they can. Tell them to make some YouTube videos, and to send their music to people in the music business.

Sorry I can't help the band or you, but for whatever it's worth, I'm a fan. Good luck.

Best,
Dave

I'm not going to say this to Buzz, because I don't want to make any more promises to my friends that I might not be able to keep, but I actually think the best thing I can do for Taxadurmee right now is to keep working on my movie and on my big idea. If I actually get into the entertainment business, *that's* when I'll be able to help my friends. Especially the talented ones.

I saved this in Dave Motts's email account. I'm not going to do anything with it right now, because I don't want it to look like Dave Motts finally wrote back on the exact day that Brianna yelled at me.

Next I'm going to do my homework. I'm getting so much done today. Staying off the internet really works. It's a miracle. Nice work, Seany.

Okay. Homework. Here I go. Stay away from the laptop. Okay. In five minutes, I absolutely promise I'm going to start my homework. After one very, very quick look at Dan Welch's email.

Finally! Something from Hank Hollywood! No. From Hank Hollywood's assistant. Kendra.

To: Dan Welch Management
From: Hank Hollywood Assist.

Dear Mr. Welch,

We are updating Hank's database, and we're missing a few pieces of information. At your earliest convenience, would you or your assistant send us the following:

—the phone number for Dan Welch Management

—the street address for Dan Welch Management

—the logline for *A Week with Your Grandparents*

Thank you in advance.

Best,

Kendra _____

Executive Assistant to Hank Hollywood

I'm confused. There's nothing about setting up a meeting to talk about the big idea. Why not? What's a logline? Why do they want Dan Welch's address and phone number?

I don't know what to do, but my five minutes are up. I'm going to keep my promise and do my homework. We'll figure this out later.

chapter 16

School today was . . . school. I still can't believe how long each day is, but knowing all my homework was done actually felt good. I turned in my story. Miss Meglis gave me a fake mad look when I handed it to her, but then she smiled. I smiled too, because I think she's going to like that story. And she's still my favorite teacher.

Brianna ignored me all day. She ignores a lot of people, but usually not me. I decided to ignore her ignoring, because I know I'm going to bring in the letter from Dave Motts tomorrow. Anyway, she isn't thinking about me. She's "In a Relationship."

On my way home, I stopped and said hello to

Baxter, who was outside his house. "Sorry, Baxter. I have to go home. I have a date with destiny." You can get away with saying things like that to an animal.

I was happy no one was home. I grabbed some lemonade and pretzels and ran up to my room. I opened my laptop and read the email from Hank Hollywood's office again.

I wonder if Kendra is the same assistant that Martin Manager heard asking questions about me at lunch in the commissary. By the way, I finally looked up commissary. It means a lot of different things, but one of them is "a lunchroom, especially in a motion-picture studio." I'm sure it's nicer than a school cafeteria. I'll probably want to eat there.

I looked up logline. It's a brief summary of a story that will get someone interested in it. What would the logline be for *A Week with Your Grandparents*?

A brother and sister find out their grandparents are a lot more interesting than they ever thought they were.

Not bad. Not great. Too many theys.

Why do they even *want* the logline? We weren't trying to sell them the movie. We only mentioned the name of it so Hank Hollywood would know we were already in the business. Why aren't they asking Dan Welch about my big idea?

Maybe Hank Hollywood is more interested in movies than in big ideas.

Or maybe he's only interested in things that other people are already interested in.

He doesn't even know that Ashley, Devin, or Eva is interested in it, too. This could actually be good. A three-way bidding war.

Chris, who's 15, and Chloe, who's 12, use Grandpa's virtual reality time machine to spend time with their grandparents back when they were teenagers.

This isn't so easy. Would I want to see the movie if I read that logline? Maybe, but it leaves out so much of what's cool about the movie.

In the Skype meeting with Stefanie, one of the Directors of Development, I don't remember which one, said the idea was "edgy." I like the sound of that word. Let's look it up. It means "bold, provocative, or unconventional." I like it. I'm going to use it.

Wait. Do we even *want* to tell Hank Hollywood's company the logline? Do we want them to bid on the movie? They're the ones I want to work with on my big idea. Would working with them on two things be too distracting for them?

I guess they're used to working on a lot of things at once. They make lots of movies and TV shows, and they also publish books and magazines and do plays and music and theme parks. That's what makes them perfect for my big idea, because you can use it on all those different things.

Okay, Kendra asked for Dan Welch's address, his phone number, and the logline. But like Thorny Rosen says, "You never get everything you want."

To: Hank Hollywood Assist.

From: Dan Welch Management

Dear Kendra,

A Week with Your Grandparents—An edgy family comedy where a virtual reality time machine lets you meet your grandparents when they were young and cool.

Best,

Dan

Dinner with my parents was fun. Mom is off tomorrow, Dad's working on two jobs, both with non-annoying clients, and I'm not worrying anymore about Dave Motts or Hank Hollywood or my short story. Everyone's in a good mood.

"You know, I've been thinking about your second honeymoon. You two should go soon."

They looked at each other like this was the best idea in the world.

Then my dad said, "Just the *two* of us?" He was making fun of me, because when we talked about this before, for like half a second, I thought I would be going too.

"Beg me all you want, but I'm not going with you. I'll stay with Grandma."

Now they looked at each other like, "Who *is* this kid?"

My dad said, "Really? I thought you didn't want to." Thorny is his mom.

"I didn't, but now I do. Just for a long weekend. Is three days okay?"

My mom said, "Three days is great. Will you be flying to Florida all by yourself?"

"No. There will almost definitely be other people in the plane. Plus the pilot. I'll be fine."

They made me call Thorny myself to ask her. I think they think if I can't get through a phone call with her, I shouldn't go for a visit.

She picked up after two rings. She has phones all over her condo.

GRANDMA:	It's about time you called.
ME:	Hi, Grandma. It's not Dad.
	It's me.
GRANDMA:	Oh. It comes up Jack Rosen.
ME:	I know.
GRANDMA:	Hi, Mr. Adorable.
ME:	Hi.
GRANDMA:	It isn't my birthday, is it?
ME:	I don't think so.

I actually don't know when her birthday is. My mom hands me a card and I sign it.

GRANDMA:	To what do I owe this pleasure?
ME:	I was thinking it might be fun if I came to Florida to visit you for a few days.
GRANDMA:	Really?
ME:	Yeah.
GRANDMA:	With your parents?
ME:	No. Just me.

GRANDMA: Really?!

ME: Yeah. It might be fun.

GRANDMA: What if it isn't?

No one said anything for a second.

GRANDMA: I'm kidding. Yes. Come. Do
           not buy a ticket. I have
           miles out the wazoo.

I don't want to know what that means.

           Email me the dates and I'll
           take care of the ticket.

ME: Okay.

GRANDMA: You're not a vegetarian or
           something, are you?

ME: No. That's Rachael (my cousin).

GRANDMA: Good. It doesn't matter
           anyway. We'll go to Publix
           when you get here. Put your
           father on.

ME:	I think he's out on a job.
GRANDMA:	I think he told you to say that. Life goes on. See you soon, sweetheart. Mmm-*mmm*.

That was the sound of a hug. Grandma is the world's hardest hugger. It's actually a little too much. Maybe when I'm there, I can teach her how to do it softer.

chapter 17

I printed out the email from Dave Motts and brought it to school today. I could have just forwarded it to Buzz, but I don't think he ever uses email. I actually brought in two copies, one for Brianna and one for Doug.

I feel a little funny pretending I'm not Dave Motts. I know. I've been pretending I'm not Dan Welch for a while now. But not to other kids. Not even to other grown-ups that live in my town. This feels different.

I don't want to get into a whole big thing with Brianna, so I didn't talk to her in any of my classes, which she probably didn't notice, because she was still ignoring me. I waited until lunch, and then I did something I almost never do. I went to the cafeteria.

Brianna always sits at the same table, in the same seat. There are always a bunch of girls sitting with her. I'm not sure if they're the same girls every day, but whoever they are, Brianna is usually talking and they're listening.

She saw me walking over, and she kept talking. I got there and stood next to her. The other girls all looked at me. Finally, Brianna stopped talking and turned to me. "Yes?"

"Can you give this to Buzz for me?" I handed her the paper with the email printed on it, folded in half. She took it from me, opened the paper, and started reading it.

As I walked away, I said, "Thanks."

I saw Ethan sitting by himself. I went over to say hi. He knows I don't like the cafeteria, so he never expects me to eat lunch with him. I sat down for a second and took out the other copy of the email. One thing I like about being with Ethan is we don't really have to talk.

Ethan's quiet. *Very* quiet. And I know you won't

believe this, but so am I. You probably think I never shut up, and if you've seen my podcasts, you know it's easy for me to just start talking to people. It is, but remember, I'm talking to them about *them*, not about *me*. Most of the time, I don't talk.

I looked around the cafeteria. I said to Ethan, "Do you see Doug?" Even sitting down, he can see a lot more than I can. He pointed.

"Thanks. See you later." That was me. Ethan didn't say a word that whole time.

I walked over to Doug, who was sitting with his friends.

"Hey, Doug. This came from Dave Motts."

I handed him the piece of paper and started to leave.

"Wait."

"I can't right now, but I'll see you later."

I actually might *not* see him later. We don't really have classes together. We did in elementary school, but now the smarter kids are in different classes from the not-as-smart kids.

I went into the boys' room and texted Buzz.

Got an email from Dave Motts. Gave it to Brianna

and Doug. Talk later.

I sent it, and the next second, I heard an announcement.

"Sean Rosen, please report to the principal's office."

Uh-oh.

Thank goodness I'm not still in the cafeteria. As soon as the assistant principal said my name in the announcement, I'm sure all the kids went "WOOO!" and made other obnoxious sounds, and I would have been embarrassed, which would make me turn red, which would make everyone make fun of me even more.

I stopped for a second before I left the boys' room to think about what I might have done. You're not supposed to text during school. Do they have cameras in here? No. You don't get called to the principal's office for turning in a short story a day late, which is good because Mr. Parsons would need a much bigger office. I guess I'll find out in a minute.

When I walked into the office, Trish said, "Hi, Sean. Sorry about the announcement, but I never know where you are during lunch. Only where you're not."

"I actually went there today. I'm not in trouble?"

"No. Not at all."

"Good. So . . . the track team didn't exactly work out."

"I know. I ran into Mr. Obester."

"What did he say?"

"Oh, you know. Nothing bad. Just that it wasn't your cup of tea."

"He said 'cup of tea'?"

"No. You know, the sports version of that. Anyway, that's old news. Do you know any other Sean Rosens?"

"*Are* there any?"

"I don't know. Sometimes people Google themselves and find other people with the same name."

"Now that you mention it, I think there *are* a few other Sean Rosens. Why?"

"I got a call. I didn't see her number because it was transferred to me. She said, 'I'm calling about a student of yours.'"

"Is that what her voice sounded like?"

"No. I don't know. I can't do impressions. Why do I even try? Anyway, then she said, 'His name is Sean Rosen.' And I said, 'Who am I speaking with?' She didn't answer me. She just said, 'He's a very creative student.' And I said, 'If you can just give me a number to call you back—' Then she said thank you and hung up. Sean, do you know who it was?"

"I have no idea. Probably just someone who saw my podcasts."

"Your *what*?"

I told Trish about my podcasts. We watched a little bit of the dog one. I said I don't want to make a big thing of it at school, because other kids might think they're stupid.

She said she was going to call my parents about the lady who called. I said, "You can call them if you want to, but they already know about my podcasts, and I don't think there's anything else to tell."

Actually, I *do* have an idea who it was.

———————

It was the end of the day, and I was waiting outside school for Ethan. He's smarter about computer stuff than I am. Kids kept asking me why I'm in trouble. I couldn't think of a good answer, so I said, "I'm not supposed to talk about it." Now they *really* want to know.

"Hey, Ethan!" He came over. "If someone liked my podcast, and wanted to find out where I live, could they do that?"

"Depends. Is your domain registration public or private?"

"I don't know. How do you know?"

"Does your phone have internet?"

"No."

"We can check in the library."

We went back into school, and on one of the library computers, Ethan went to a site called Whois.net. He typed in SeanRosen.com, and there it was: the exact address of my house, plus my cell phone number. I guess I gave it to them when I got my website.

I don't know why, but it felt a little scary seeing it there. Like if you hated my podcast, you could come to my town and throw eggs at my house. Or keep calling me and not say anything and use up all of my minutes.

But I don't think the lady who called my school was someone who hated my podcast. I think it was Kendra or someone else who works for Hank Hollywood. First they tried to find out where Dan Welch lives, and now they're trying to find out where *I* live.

But why, Kendra??? Please! Do what Dan Welch asked you. Set up a Skype meeting for me and Hank Hollywood, then you can just *ask* me where I live. I'll tell you. Probably.

Anyway, when I get home, I'm changing my domain registration to private. I think it costs more, but I don't want people throwing eggs at my house.

chapter 18

I came home from school and checked Dan Welch's email. I saw something I never saw before. The number 3 next to his inbox. He has three new emails. Things are happening. I guess I'll just read them in order. Some people would open all three emails and take a quick look to see what they say. Like this one girl I know. Whenever she gets a new book, she reads the last few pages first. She can't stand not knowing how it ends.

I never want to know how something ends until the end. And if you're reading something I wrote, I never want you to know how it ends until the end. Miss Meglis says a good story always has a beginning, a middle, and an end, and my advice is to read it in that exact order.

That's what I'm going to do with these emails. But first I'm going to change the domain registration on my website from public to private, so I don't forget.

Making SeanRosen.com private was very easy to do. It only costs about twelve dollars a year. My parents gave me a debit card to use for emergencies. I don't know if this counts as an emergency, but it *is* a little weird that someone I don't know called my school. Anyway, I'll give my parents the twelve dollars. They don't have to pay for my website.

Okay. That's done. I can look at the emails.

To: Dan Welch Management
From: Stefanie V. President

Dear Dan,

I can't believe Ashley had the nerve to write to you. Finally! We know which Director of Development it was. I still can't believe she left, and now she's trying to take something that's rightfully mine.

I know what you're thinking. I used to work for Hank Hollywood, and now he and I compete for projects. That's true, of course, but when I left there, I didn't abruptly abandon the studio (with *no* notice). And on my way out, I didn't try to grab most of my boss's goodies (like Sean's movie) and cram them into my counterfeit Gucci bag. That's exactly what she's doing. Do I sound angry? I am.

And just for the record, I was Hank's *intern*. Ashley was paid an unbelievably high salary to learn every single thing she knows—from *me*. Then she leaves without even the hint of a thank you, plundering the relationships I took so long to build.

Dan, I'm sure you've had clients leave you. I know this happens all the time in our business. It doesn't make it hurt any less.

Okay. Enough wound licking. You're your own man, and Sean is his own boy, and I know that together you'll make the decision that's right for him as he begins his career.

But as someone who knows you well (my best to your wife and kids), who cherishes our working relationship, I must say this to you. Do *not* let that woman near any artistic property that you care about. She is not to be trusted.

I know this is one of those emails I should write and never send, but I also know that you'll take it in the spirit of friendship. Call me.

xo,
S

_____

To: Dan Welch Management
From: Ashley _____

Dear Dan,

I can't tell you how happy I am to be sending you this email. I have been desperately wanting to be in touch with you about Sean Rosen's *A Week with Your Grandparents*. (The title actually sounds good that way.)

I have been in love with this project since the day Sean pitched it to us on Skype. I was devastated (but not surprised) that Stefanie President wasn't able to make a deal with you. I had been lobbying to be put in charge of the project, and when her attempt to play "hardball" in your negotiation failed, I gave a silent cheer for Sean through my tears of disappointment.

Flash forward! I was offered a production job at _____ a different big Hollywood studio, also very famous, which I had to think about for a grand total of five seconds. Any studio that would let Sean Rosen go so easily is not a place I'm betting my future on.

Dan, you know this business. We hear ten pitches a day, from the biggest and brightest names in Hollywood. When someone cuts through all the noise and tells us a story we actually want to see . . . right now . . . with our families and our best friends, we know it immediately. Well, some of us do.

And when you hear a story like that from someone just beginning his career, you can imagine making movie after movie with this bright light named Sean. That's why I'm writing.

I truly do not understand my former company's conduct and lack of vision. I'm sorry you had to experience that, but it's a new day, with a studio that values young talent and will do whatever we have to do to make this happen.

I was having trouble finding your info, Dan. Thank goodness I remembered Sean's podcasts, which I love, Love, LOVE!! I want a donut! And a dog! And a stamp!

I have to warn you. There's a very odd person whose name also happens to be Dan Welch, who is claiming he's your close friend and "the representor" (whatever that is) of both you and Sean Rosen. Steer clear of that guy!

Let's make a deal. Love to Sean. Call me. Soon.

Best,

Ashley

_____

To: Dan Welch Management
From: Dan Welch

Hey Dan Welch,

Hows your week? Mine is going good, thanks to
the biz we're both in. No, not collectibles (least
I hope not - I don't need the competish). Show
biz! You will not beleive what someone just paid
me for a fork used by the one and only Miss
Miley Cyrus.

Usually you need there autograph for the big
bucks, but if you ever tried to sign a fork,
you know. You cant. But I had a picture of
Miley holding the fork and a signed affadavid
from the waiter, which was fine for my rich

customer, who is now the proud owner of The Miley Fork.

I didnt hear back from you about what we should tell that movie person. I figure your busy. How many people do you manage anyway? Since your busy and we already got the fish on the line, I wrote and told them we'ed be back to them soon.

Dan, I been selling people stuff for a long time now and we dont want to lose our mojo on this sale, now do we? I think we're good for now, but think about our next move and let me know soon, ok? You got my number, right?

Hey, if Sean ever wants to do a Collectibles podcast, I'm in.

Peace and carrots,
Dan K. Welch (K for Kelvin. I know.)

"Sean! Dinner!"

chapter 19

In one way, I'm glad it's time to eat. I'm hungry, and those emails are just . . . I don't know . . . too much. All these grown-ups trying really hard to talk me into doing something. Stefanie and Ashley having a fight, and the fight is over me. I know. I wanted a bidding war. Now I have one. Now what do I do?

It's exciting, but it makes me think of something my dad says to me. "Seany, you're in over your head." Like when you're swimming, and you stop, and you think you can stand on the bottom. But then when you try, your head goes under the water. It's deeper than you thought it was. But you don't know *how* deep. Should you try to touch the bottom, or just turn around and swim back to where it's safe? I can't decide right now.

I went downstairs.

"It's just us tonight. Your dad has Boys' Night."

This isn't good. If it's just my mom and me, she'll know something's going on, and it'll be hard not to answer her questions.

I guess I could tell her. Why wouldn't I want to? I feel bad keeping a secret from my parents. I actually don't think of it as a secret. It's just my own thing. She doesn't tell *me* everything either, and to tell you the truth, I wouldn't want her to.

"How was your day?"

It took me a second to remember she was talking to me.

"Oh. Good. How about you?"

She was busy at the stove making sure everything was ready and hot. That's the only way I got away with that answer. If she was looking at me, she would have read my mind by now.

"My day was good. We sent three patients home. The new nurse manager started."

"What's she like?" The longer I can keep her talking, the better.

She brought our plates to the table. It's some kind of fish that actually looks really good, and string beans and those little red potatoes. She poured herself a glass of wine and poured me a mixture of cran-grape juice and seltzer. It's like soda, but a little healthier.

"Now *what* did you ask me? What the new nurse manager is like? I would tell you if I thought you were even slightly interested."

"I *am*. I swear."

"Why are you interested?"

"I want you to like your job. And you thought the old nurse manager was annoying."

"She was. I think I'm going to like this new one."

"Good. I'm glad to hear it."

She was laughing at me without laughing. "Thanks, Sean. What else do you want to know about my fascinating life?"

"What did you have for lunch today?"

"A yogurt. An orange. And a little bag of cashews."

"Interesting."

"No it's not. You get one more question, then *I* go."

I better make it good. "Why did you and Dad only have one kid?"

She gave me a look like "Where did *that* come from?," but she didn't say anything.

"Was it like you had *me* and you saw what it was like, and then you decided, 'Let's not do *that* again'?"

"You don't actually think that, do you?"

"I don't know. I have no idea. That's why I asked you."

"Why we only had one kid?"

"Yeah. You don't have to tell me."

She looked at me like she was deciding if she wanted to or not.

"Did you ever *try* to have another kid?"

"No, Sean. We didn't. Okay. Here's what happened. I can't believe we're having this conversation, but . . . we are. Like you said, we tried it once . . . having a kid, I mean . . . and it was you. And yes, we saw what it was like. We loved it. Completely loved it. We couldn't imagine ever being happier than we were. So we decided to stick with a good thing."

I thought about all that.

Then she said, "Do you *wish* you had a brother or sister?"

"No. No! Do not get pregnant. I mean, you can if you want to. But no. I like it the way we have it now too."

"Good."

"Good. Weren't you going to ask *me* something?"

I don't know what made me so brave all of a sudden. I really do like my parents. And they're pretty honest with me. Okay, whatever question my mom asks me right now, I'm going to tell her the truth. I swear.

She's thinking. This is actually exciting. She probably won't say, "Do you have a secret identity?" Or "Are three different Hollywood studios interested in you and your ideas?" But it doesn't matter. Whatever she asks, I'm answering.

"What made you change your mind about staying with Grandma?"

Close. I told you she's good. Okay. I swore.

"Three things. I want to find out more about Grandpa. I want you and Dad to have a good honeymoon. And I want to do research for something I'm writing."

"Okay. Thanks. What are you writing?"

"I'll show you when it's finished. I promise. Is it okay if I get back to work? I have a lot to do."

"Okay."

"I can help clean up."

"Get outa here." (She was doing an imitation of my dad.)

"Okay. Thanks, Mom."

chapter 20

I sat down at my desk. I have a lot of different places in my room where I sometimes work—the floor, the bed, the chair—but when there's serious business to figure out, like all these emails, I usually do it at my desk.

I see that I got three texts while I was downstairs.

By by dave mots

U tryed

Tuf luk 4 yor moovy

Buzz. For a minute I got confused. My "moovy" is doing fine. In fact, I think there's going to be a bidding war for it. But then I remembered that Buzz thinks "dave mots" was my manager, and now that he's moving to Paraguay, that's it for my moovy. Anyway, Buzz doesn't sound mad. Good. I have enough to worry about.

Okay. What do we do? Stefanie, Ashley, and Collectibles all want Dan Welch to call them. Sorry. He's not going to. I once tried using Ethan as Dan Welch on the phone. Ethan sounds like a grown-up when he talks, and I wrote down exactly what I wanted him to say, but he always sounded like he was reading it.

I could try to hire an actor, but I think if you're an actor, you probably don't live around here. Anyway, I don't trust anyone to be Dan Welch except Dan Welch.

Stefanie is really mad at Ashley, and says I shouldn't be in business with her. Stefanie also says I shouldn't be in business with Hank Hollywood. I like Stefanie, but I think she might be saying those things about the others because *she* wants to be the one who gets *A Week with Your Grandparents*.

But we don't even know yet if Hank Hollywood wants the movie, and we only just heard from Ashley. Dan Welch isn't ready to write back to Stefanie yet.

My phone beeped. It's a text from Brianna.

Gave Buzz the email from Dave Motts.

I guess Buzz and Brianna aren't together right now, or she would have known that he already texted me. I'm a little tempted not to text her back because she's been pretty mean to me lately. But she's my friend, and I like being friends with her when she's not being mean to me.

Thanks.

Okay, now Ashley. I listened to the recording of the Skype meeting again, and she was the one who used the word "edgy." You can't really tell from the recording, but from her email it sounds like she really loves *A Week with Your Grandparents*. I guess we have to find out how *much* she loves it.

To: Ashley _____
From: Dan Welch Management

Dear Ashley,

Thank you for all the nice things you said about Sean. I'm glad you like his podcasts. I'll let him know. I want a donut, too.

We appreciate the warning about the other Dan Welch. He is not our "representor."

Can you tell us what you have in mind for *A Week with Your Grandparents*?

Best,
Dan

And what about Collectibles? Now that Ashley found the right Dan Welch, we don't need him anymore. But he doesn't know that. He still wants to be in the middle of everything, and he doesn't want us to lose our "mojo."

I wasn't sure if that's a real word or if he meant something else and just spelled it wrong. Miss Meglis would be happy if she knew how many words I'm looking up.

One site says your mojo is your magic spell. I don't really believe in magic spells, even though they were fun in Harry Potter. I wouldn't want to use a magic spell to convince someone to like my movie. I don't think we have to.

The other definition of mojo is self-confidence. I know that it's possible to lose your self-confidence. Once I accidentally signed "Sean" to one of Dan Welch's emails to Stefanie. I thought my career was over. I couldn't stop saying mean things to myself. I lost my mojo. I'm glad I have it back.

Collectibles acts like he has a lot of mojo, but it might not be the kind of mojo we need.

To: Dan Welch
From: Dan Welch Management

Dear Dan,

I just wanted to let you know that everything is taken care of with Sean's movie. Thanks for offering to help.

Congratulations for selling The Miley Fork.

Best,
Dan

chapter 21

At the end of each school day, we have announcements. They come through the speakers into every room in the school. Last year they tried an experiment of letting students read the announcements. It only lasted a few weeks, and I got to do it one day. It was kind of fun, but I kept wanting to change things or add things to make it more entertaining.

They stopped it because some days you'd have a kid who can't read that well or doesn't speak that clearly or can't stop laughing, so you weren't really sure what the announcement was. One day a lot of people went to the wrong town for a basketball game, and that was the end.

I actually think the real reason the experiment ended is that our assistant principal *loves* making announcements. She wanted her job back. Sometimes I think she makes up announcements so she can talk even longer. I'm not going to tell you everything she announced today, because you'll fall asleep, but here are the two important things:

"The yearbook staff will meet today immediately after school in the Publication Room. There is absolutely no reason to be late."

I'm sure she added that last part herself. I'm one of the editors, and that doesn't sound like something that Mr. Hollander, our advisor, would ever say.

"Directly following these announcements, all seventh graders will be handed information packets and permission slips for the seventh-grade class trip. As you may know, the last three seventh-grade classes did not *have* a trip. We are conditionally restoring this privilege. Please behave."

Of course everyone wants to know where the trip is to. People started guessing. "Disney

World!" "Washington, D.C.!" "Paris!" (That was Brianna.) Then we got the handouts. None of the guesses were even close. It's a place I never heard of—Pine Tree Wilderness Retreat. The minute I saw the words "sleeping bags," I knew I wasn't going. I don't sleep in a bag.

Walking in the hall after class, I said that to Ethan. I guess I like the sound of it.

"Sorry. I don't sleep in a bag."

"Why not? It's fun."

"Are you kidding?"

"You don't sleep on the *ground* in a sleeping bag. We'll be on cots. In cabins."

"*You'll* be on cots in cabins."

"You're not gonna go?"

"No. I like a nice bed in a nice room, all by myself."

"Didn't you ever go to camp?"

"Not sleepaway camp. Did you?"

"Once. It's really fun."

"Ethan, I believe you. I mean, I believe that *you* think it's fun. I don't believe that *I* would think it's fun."

"Have you ever tried it?"

"No, and I don't want to."

He looked kind of sad. I said, "What?"

"If you're not going, I'm not gonna go."

"Why not? Ethan, you *like* the wilderness. You should definitely go."

"Yeah. Okay." He started to walk away.

"Wait! Why don't you come to the yearbook meeting with me?"

"No."

"But you're such a good photographer."

He didn't say anything. He just sort of waved and walked away. It wasn't even a wave, actually. He just sort of stuck out his hand as he walked away.

"What's *his* problem?" It was Brianna.

"Oh, I want him to join the yearbook, and he won't."

"Why?"

"He just won't."

"No. I mean why do you want him to join?"

"He's a really good photographer."

"He *is*? How do you even know?"

"He's been working on my podcasts with me."

"He *has*?"

"Yeah. Have you seen my podcast lately?"

"No. Sorry. I've been kind of busy."

She means Buzz. I don't want to talk about him with her. I guess *she* does, though.

"Buzz is *so* creative, don't you think?"

"I like his songs a lot."

"Yeah, of course. But other things too."

I didn't say anything, but that never stops Brianna.

"Like, for example, his spelling."

I couldn't help myself. I laughed. "Yeah. His spelling is very creative." I had to change the subject. "You're not going on that class trip, are you?"

"Of course I am. So are you."

"Brianna, did you look at that handout? Wilderness. Sleeping bags. No wifi. No phones or devices allowed."

"We'll see about that."

We walked into the Publication Room. Brianna is also an editor of the yearbook. The fashion editor. She said, "Hi, Mr. Hollander. Nice tie. The seventh-grade trip is going to be in the yearbook, right?"

He thought for a second. "Yes. It's a major event. You'll want to remember it."

"Can Sean and I be in charge of that layout?"

"No!" I actually whispered that to Brianna. I don't know if Mr. Hollander heard.

It's been a little strange being around Mr. Hollander ever since I came up with Dan Welch, because they remind me of each other. They're both super-nice guys, and they talk almost the same way. I mean in my head. I mean Dan Welch. He only chats and emails, but in my head I hear him talking, and he sounds like Mr. H.

"Are you up for that, Sean?"

"I guess."

"Good. I'm sure you two will do a stellar job."

After the meeting, I thought about Ethan. I should tell him I'm going to Wilderness Torture, or whatever it's called. I would text him, but I don't even know if he has a phone. I've never seen him with one. We just talk (or don't talk) when we see each other at school, or at my house, or wherever we're doing the podcast.

I guess I'll see him tomorrow morning when he comes over to work on the podcast. *If* he comes. I wonder if he's mad at me. I actually think he is. Maybe I should go to his house right now to tell him. I'm pretty sure I remember where it is.

But he might not want me to come there. It was pretty strange the last time. I wonder if it will be more strange or less strange now that I know about his brother.

Yeah. I should go there. Ethan only had about five minutes of looking forward to the class trip before I wrecked it for him. I should tell him as soon as possible that we're going after all.

I stopped for a second to look up the name of Pine Tree Wilderness Retreat so I don't call it Wilderness Torture. Then I walked over to Ethan's.

I recognize his house. There's a car in the driveway. I'm a little nervous, but so what. I ring the doorbell. The lady who comes to the door looks a little older than my mom.

"Hi. Are you Ethan's mom?"

"Sean." That's Ethan. He must have heard the doorbell. Now he's standing behind his mom.

"Hi. I'm Sean."

"Hello."

Ethan stepped around his mom and came outside. "Come on, let's go in the back."

His mom was still standing there. I waved good-bye to her as we walked away. Sometimes I feel like The Visitor from the Friendly Planet.

"Is it okay that I came over?"

"Yeah. We can try a science experiment."

I had no idea what he meant. The backyard is kind of a mess. Like the last people who had the house stopped taking care of it a long time ago, and Ethan's family never started. There's some grass, but not like a lawn, and a few rusty chairs. Ethan pointed to an old seesaw.

"I can't get either of my parents to go on this thing with me."

I looked at him and looked at the seesaw and cracked up. Ethan weighs a lot more than I do. Double. No. More than double.

"Ethan, if *I* sit on this end, and then *you* sit on that end, I can actually fly home."

"No. I think we can do it."

"What? Both break our heads?"

"No. Balance. I think the wood is pretty strong."

"You *think* so?"

"Yeah."

"Why do you think so?"

"It just looks strong. Wait."

He pulled some old cushions off the rusty chairs and put them under one end of the seesaw.

"You sit there."

I started to take off my backpack.

"No. Leave it on. We'll need the weight of your books."

"Ethan . . ."

"Come on, you'll be fine."

I sat down on the seesaw. My end isn't touching the ground anymore because it's resting on the cushions. I'm sure I don't look happy.

"See? *This* is what I'm like. Why would you even *want* to go to Wilderness . . . whatever it's called . . . with someone like *me*?"

Ethan stood on the other side of the seesaw, near the middle. He lifted his leg over it, then looked at me, then looked at the seesaw. He moved back a little bit, then sat down very, very gently, with his feet still on the ground.

I started rising up in the air, very slowly. When I got higher than Ethan was, he brought me back down. Then he moved closer to the middle, and he started again. No one said anything.

I rose up again, and this time Ethan very slowly took one foot off the ground . . . then the other. I didn't go flying. We're balanced.

"Nice." That was me.

"See?"

"I *do* see."

We stayed balanced. If either of us moved, even a little bit, we would start to rock, but we were always able to get it steady again.

"I'm sorry I'm such a wimp about this class trip."

He didn't say anything.

"It's not just the wilderness part. I'm just not . . . I don't know . . . like a sleepover kind of kid. I don't like . . . doing all that stuff with strangers. Or even kids I know."

He still didn't say anything.

"Anyway, I'm going." The seesaw wobbled.

"You *are*?"

"Yes. Brianna is making me. We're covering it for the yearbook."

"Okay. Good."

"I'm not so sure about that."

"It'll be fun."

"It will?"

"Yeah. I'll keep an eye on you."

"Good. Maybe both eyes." I just remembered how scared I got in the woods right next to Brianna's house. "Did your family used to go camping or something?"

"No. Just me. Skip was always on teams, and my parents were like the world's biggest sports parents. My dad was always one of the coaches, and my mom would go to all the games, and bake things and sell them with the other moms."

"So all of that stopped."

"Right. Anyway, when the three of them were

going to tournaments out of town, I would stay with my Uncle Neil. My aunt and cousins don't like camping, so it would only be him and me. Uncle Neil is like a mountain lion or something. He loves to be outside. He taught me how to do a lot of stuff."

"Do they live where you used to live?"

"Yeah."

"Well, you'll see them again."

"I guess. Are you ready to come down?" We were still balancing on the seesaw.

"Yeah."

"What kind of landing do you want?"

"These cushions look okay."

"So I can just jump off?"

"Yeah. Go ahead."

I came down fast, but it didn't hurt at all.

chapter 22

There's been so much going on that I haven't had time to work on my screenplay. I think I should. I'm going to Florida soon to visit Thorny. I want to have my questions ready for her about the character of Grandma in the movie. The other reason I have to work on the screenplay is that it looks like there actually might be a bidding war for *A Week with Your Grandparents*. When one of the studios wins, I want them to be able to start making the movie right away.

It's Sunday morning, and my mom's at church. She goes on Christmas, Easter, and sometimes on Sunday when she's not working. Once in a while I go with her, but today I knew I wanted to work on the movie. My dad is asleep. He likes to sleep late on Sundays.

I took my laptop and the printed-out screenplay so far and got comfortable in my favorite spot on the couch in our Biscuit-colored family room. If we had a dog, he'd be there sitting with me while I work.

Okay, so here's where we are in the story. Chris and Chloe's parents go on a second honeymoon, and they make the kids stay with their grandparents. The kids find out that Grandpa is an inventor. They both try his virtual reality time machine, which lets you spend time with anyone, on any day in their past. You just need some of their DNA, which you can get from their spit or their hair.

Chloe meets Grandpa when he was seventeen and discovers that he was a cool, nice kid. Chris meets Grandma when she was his age, fifteen. She isn't exactly nice to him, but he thinks she's very, very interesting.

This time they're going to switch grandparents. Chris is going to visit Grandpa's past. That's the scene I'm writing today.

GRANDPA'S WORK ROOM
Grandma and Chloe are out shopping,
and Chris and Grandpa are in the
basement, where he keeps the virtual
reality time machine. It's late in the
morning, but you can't really tell
since there aren't any windows. There's
a lot of stuff in the room: wires,
tools, metal parts of things, but each
thing is in a certain place, and it
looks like Grandpa can find whatever
he needs very easily.

CHRIS:	Did you always like science?
GRANDPA:	I did. How about you?
CHRIS:	It's sort of interesting, but . . . I don't really get how most of it works. Science makes me feel stupid sometimes.
GRANDPA:	That's not stupid. That's just the way it is, even for scientists. There's so much

in the world that's almost impossible to understand. We all just guess, and most of our guesses are wrong. You can work on something for years, but there's usually something you forget. Oh. I forgot to tell Grandma to get oatmeal.

Chris pulls out his phone.

CUT TO: A close-up of Chris's fingers texting Chloe:

GRANDPA NEEDS OATMEAL.

He sends it, and a few seconds later Chloe texts back:

K

GRANDPA: Like *that*. Whoever figured out how to do *that* was really smart, but I guarantee you, they made a

lot of mistakes along the
way. Okay, Mr. Chris. Where
in my past are we sending
you?

CHRIS: I don't know. (thinks
about it) How old were you
when you met Grandma?

GRANDPA: Let's see . . . I was . . .
twenty-five.

CHRIS: Was Grandma back then . . .
you know . . . like she is
now?

GRANDPA: Yes. Grandma has always been
Grandma, and will always be
Grandma. Well, you just met
her when she was fifteen.
What was she like?

CHRIS: Just like Grandma. I want to
meet *you* before you met *her.*

GRANDPA: Why?

CHRIS: I don't know . . . I only
know you two together, and
you're always . . . I don't

know . . . the quiet one.
That's why we never knew
you were an inventor.

GRANDPA: Well . . . that plus
the fact that you never
asked me anything.

CHRIS: That's true. I'm sorry.

GRANDPA: Tokyo!

CHRIS: What?

GRANDPA: When I was in the Army in
Korea, I went to Tokyo on
leave. It was definitely
not quiet.

CHRIS: Let's go there!

GRANDPA: Okay. But remember, it won't
be you and me going on an
adventure together. You'll
be *there* with me, but I
won't know who you *are*.

CHRIS: Right. Because you'll only
be . . . *how* old?

GRANDPA: Twenty.

CHRIS: And you won't have a

grandson yet. Will I know who *you* are?

GRANDPA: Good question. (thinks)
I *think* so. But let me get you a picture just to be sure. I might even have one from the night I'm thinking of.

CHRIS: What night?

GRANDPA: New Year's Eve, 1952.

CHRIS: Yes! We're par-ty-ing in Tok-y-o!

CUT TO: An old photo of three smiling twenty-year-old guys wearing U.S. Army uniforms. The camera zooms out and now we see that Chris is holding the photo as he sits inside the virtual reality time machine, a metal box that covers him from his head down to his waist. When Grandpa talks to Chris inside the machine, he does it by pushing buttons on the side that say TALK and LISTEN.

GRANDPA: Remember, you won't have
that picture with you in
Tokyo. It's *virtual* reality.
It feels completely real,
but it all happens in your
mind. And even though I'll
be here in the basement
with you, I won't know what
you're experiencing in Tokyo.

CHRIS: Okay. How did you ever come
up with this, Grandpa?

GRANDPA: I'll tell you some time
when you're not sitting in
a metal box. So Chris . . .
there's gonna be a lot of
American soldiers there,
and some of them . . .
well . . . it's New Year's
Eve. And they're very, very
happy to be away from the
war. So just make sure you
stick with *me*.

CHRIS: I promise. Oh, and please,

> Grandpa . . . let me *stay*
> there a little while.
> Grandma hits the stop
> button way too soon.

GRANDPA: Okay, boss.

Grandpa sets the dial on the machine to December 31, 1952. He spits on a glass slide and puts it into a slot in the machine.

GRANDPA: Ready?

CHRIS: Happy New Year!

Grandpa smiles, then hits the start button. One by one the green lights come on. SIGHT. SOUNDS. SMELL. TASTE. TOUCH. Then the little bell rings. Chris is in virtual reality.

CUT TO: TOKYO 1952. It's nighttime in a very crowded street in Tokyo.

This is the Ginza, a famous shopping and tourist area. The street is filled with Japanese people, American soldiers, bicycles, and little cars. There are lots of stores and some bars and restaurants. Some of the Japanese people are dressed in kimonos and other Japanese clothes, and some are dressed in shirts and pants and dresses. The American soldiers are wearing uniforms. Chris, dressed the same as he was in the last scene, is excited and a little scared as he looks around the crowd. He hears a voice from behind him.

SOLDIER: (to Chris) Hey kid!

Chris turns around.

SOLDIER: (to his friends) He speaks
           English. (to Chris) Are you
           lost?

Chris is a little nervous, but he comes over. Chris stares at the soldier, but he doesn't look like Grandpa at twenty.

SOLDIER: Are you English, Australian, or American?

CHRIS: American.

SOLDIER: Us too!

Two other American soldiers walk up, carrying bags from a store. Chris sees that they're the other guys in the picture, including Grandpa when he was twenty. Chris is relieved to see him.

YOUNG GRANDPA: (points to his uniform) I think he *knows* we're American. What brings you to Tokyo?

CHRIS: Oh. I don't know. Just visiting.

YOUNG GRANDPA: How do you like it here?

CHRIS:	Actually, I *just* got here.
YOUNG GRANDPA:	Today?
CHRIS:	Yeah. Just now.
YOUNG GRANDPA:	Where are your parents?
CHRIS:	Oh. Ummm . . . the hotel.
YOUNG GRANDPA:	Do they know you're out and about?
CHRIS:	Yeah. They're . . . you know . . . tired.
YOUNG GRANDPA:	I know. Long flight. So you haven't seen Tokyo at all?
CHRIS:	Nope.
YOUNG GRANDPA:	Do you like amusement parks?
CHRIS:	Love.
FIRST SOLDIER:	Not again.
YOUNG GRANDPA:	Yes. We have to. (to Chris) What's your name?

CHRIS: Chris.

YOUNG GRANDPA: We won't stay long,
                because we have to
                meet our buddies before
                midnight, but you have
                to see Hanayashiki.
                Follow me.

CHRIS: Cool!

Young Grandpa starts walking, followed
by Chris and the other two soldiers.
The street gets more and more crowded.
Chris bumps into a Japanese man.

JAPANESE MAN: (angry) 気を付けてね！
              (Japanese for "Be careful.")

CHRIS: I don't know what you just
              said, but I'm really, really,
              really sorry.

JAPANESE MAN: 私はちょうど家に帰るようにし
              ようとしています。

(Japanese for "I'm just
trying to go home.")

Chris looks around and doesn't see
Young Grandpa. There are so many
American soldiers in uniforms. We see
the crowd on the street the way Chris
sees it as he slowly looks from left
to right. Wait. There's Young Grandpa!
Chris waves, but Young Grandpa doesn't
see him. Chris tries to move through
the crowd as quickly as he can, but
it's hard to do.

KA-PLOW!!!

There's an explosion in the street
near Chris. Some people scream and
try to move out of the way. Then we
see some American soldiers laughing.

LAUGHING SOLDIER: Sorry, everyone.

Just a firecracker.
My idiot friend.

Chris, who got scared, just stands
there.

YOUNG GRANDPA: Chris!

Chris turns. Young Grandpa and two
other soldiers are up ahead to the
right.

YOUNG GRANDPA: (points, then really
loud, so Chris can
hear) THIS way. We're
taking the TRAIN. (He
points to a platform
where people are
waiting.) FOLLOW ME.

Grandpa was so loud that a lot of
people stopped to listen. That made

it possible for Chris to get through
the crowd and catch up to Grandpa and
his two soldier friends. The four of
them walk to the train platform.

YOUNG GRANDPA: (to Chris) Crazy night,
right?

CHRIS: Slightly.

YOUNG GRANDPA: (looks down the track)
Okay, here comes the
train. Just follow us.
If we get separated,
get off at Akasaka.
We'll meet on the
platform there.

There are hundreds of people waiting.
As the train pulls in, everyone moves
forward. The doors open and a lot of
people come out, but the train still
looks full.

YOUNG GRANDPA: (to Chris) Just push

your way in. Everyone
here does it. It's okay.

The crowd begins pushing into the
train. Now Grandpa and his friends are
inside the train. Chris just stands
there.

YOUNG GRANDPA: (from inside the train)
                Chris! Come on! Just
                push!

Chris can't do it. The doors start to
close.

CHRIS: *GRANDPA!!!!*

The doors are closed. As the train
leaves, we see Young Grandpa through
the train window. He heard Chris, but
he's confused. Who's Grandpa?
Chris is standing on the train platform
with about a hundred other people who

didn't get on the train. They're all Japanese.

Chris doesn't know what to do. Should he wait for the next train? What was the name of the amusement park? What was the name of the train stop? He can't remember. Will he ever find Grandpa?

Then Chris gets an idea. His phone has GPS, and he can Google the name of the amusement park. He pulls it out of his pocket. The people standing around him stare. They've never seen a cell phone. It's 1952. Which means there are no cell towers and no satellites. The phone doesn't work.

CHRIS: (to a Japanese lady) Do you speak English?

She just looks at him. She doesn't know what he said.

CHRIS: (to a Japanese man) Speak
           English? Amusement park?

Chris tries to show a roller coaster
with his hands, but the man doesn't
understand. Chris looks around for
American soldiers. Now there aren't any.

CHRIS: (yells really loud) Grandpa!

The people in the crowd all stare at
him. Chris is actually trying to tell
Grandpa at home in the basement to get
him out of the time machine, but no
one knows that.

CHRIS: (yells again) Grandpa!

There's an explosion. Chris jumps.
Everyone scatters. Someone threw a
firecracker. People start laughing,
but not Chris. He's very upset. He
doesn't know what to do.

Suddenly he hears a voice.

VOICE: Chris?

He looks around the train platform.
He doesn't know who's talking to him.

VOICE: Chris? Have you had enough?

It's Grandpa. Chris remembers he's in
the time machine.

CHRIS: Yes! Yes! Enough! Hit the
           red button!

CUT TO: GRANDPA'S WORKROOM. Chris is
inside the time machine. Grandpa hits
the red button. The machine powers
down. Grandpa opens the machine and
Chris gets out. He looks really,
really scared.

GRANDPA: Chris. What happened?

CHRIS: I . . . I got . . .

He can't talk. Just then, Grandma and
Chloe come down the stairs into the
workroom. Grandma sees Chris, who
still looks terrified. She holds out
her arms, and Chris runs over to her.
She hugs him for a long time. It takes
Chris a minute to start breathing
again. . . .

"Hey Seany!"

It took me a few seconds to realize my dad was
talking to me. I was like Chris. The movie felt so
real to me, I forgot I was in my family room.

"Banana pancakes?"

"Definitely."

I was actually glad my dad came in. I was
almost as scared as Chris. *I'm* glad to be back in
reality too.

What happens next in the movie is that
Grandma yells at Grandpa, because she always
told him he should put a panic button in the time

machine. He never wanted to because he thought it would spoil your virtual reality experience. And that's the reason she never lets anyone stay in the machine too long.

Grandma doesn't want anyone to use the time machine again, but Chloe talks her into it. After a day goes by, Chris is ready to go to the past again. But only places where he speaks the language.

The banana pancakes were amazing. It was like dessert for breakfast. Thanks, Dad.

chapter 23

To: Dan Welch Management
From: Stefanie V. President

Hi Dan,

I didn't hear back from you, and I shouldn't admit this to someone I negotiate with, but the silence was making me crazy. You start imagining things. "Does Dan think I'm just mad at Ashley because she left?"

Of course I am. Anyone would be, but I hope you don't think that's the only reason I don't think Sean should work with her. She has little to no status in this town, and she just lost her only important connection—me.

Ashley needs Sean Rosen more than Sean Rosen needs her.

But why are we even talking about her? Dan, I want to do the movie. I've *always* wanted to do the movie. You know that.

I promise, promise, promise to make it a movie Sean will love. I will personally guarantee that Sean will have a significant consultation with the screenwriter.

I can double our last offer, except for the net profits. I can give Sean 1.5 net profit points instead of 1.

Let's just do this. You know me. Sean knows me. Let's keep it in the family.

xo,

S

The doorbell rang. I wanted to think about this email, but for some reason, when the doorbell rings, I just jump up and answer it. It started when I was little, and answering the door is still my job.

It's a good thing I did, because it's Mrs. Dahlin and Baxter. Baxter started barking the second he saw me.

I went outside. I wanted to invite them in, but we weren't expecting an excited dog today, and I bet Baxter can break a lot of things really fast, especially in a place he's never been before.

"Baxter!" That's me saying hi to him. It's a little hard to describe how I sound when I say his name. On my dog podcast, I have a lot of different people saying hello to their dogs. I sound a little like some of those people, but I don't call him Bax-y Wax-y or say his name in that high "I'm talking to an animal" voice. It's more like how you say hi to a friend you're excited to see, when the friend is a dog.

"Hi, Mrs. Dahlin."

"Sean, I came over to ask you a gigantic favor."

"You want me to bring you and Mr. Dahlin a dozen donuts every day for the next four years."

"That *would* be gigantic, and *we* would be too. No. What I *meant* was, do you think you could possibly keep an eye on Baxter for a couple of days next week?"

"Yes! Wait. When?"

"Next Tuesday and Wednesday."

"Yes! I'll be back by then."

"Where are you going?"

"To see my grandmother in Florida."

"Nice."

"I hope. Anyway, yes. Definitely. What do I have to do?"

"Just feed him. Give him water. Take him out three times a day."

"During school?" Please. Please.

"Nah. Once in the morning, once when you get home, and once at night should do it."

"Okay."

"Good. I'll call your parents to make sure it's all right with them."

"Don't worry. It will be. They like me to have responsibilities."

"I'm still gonna call them. When do you get back from Florida?"

"Sunday night."

"Okay. Monday after school, just come by and I'll show you everything and give you a key. Is fifty dollars okay?"

For about five seconds I thought she meant I would have to pay them fifty dollars to be able to do all that stuff with Baxter. I was going to say yes. But no, *she'll* be paying *me*.

"Baxter . . . we're gonna have so much fun. Are you psyched? Are you psyched? I am!"

———

I went back upstairs and read Stefanie's email again. It's interesting that Dan Welch knew not to reply to her last email. It sounds like that's what got her to make a higher bid for my movie. She sweetened the pot.

I went back through Dan Welch's old emails to see what she means when she says she can double her offer. I found the fifty-page Revised Option Agreement we got from her studio's business affairs department. It was revised because the first Option Agreement wasn't going to pay me enough.

I didn't know how much people usually get paid

for movie ideas, but five hundred dollars from a big Hollywood studio sounded too low. Then I asked Martin Manager. He said they were trying to take advantage of me because I'm a kid and I would probably say yes because I want to be in the movie business.

Dan Welch wrote back to Stefanie and complained, and the next week they sent me a new contract, which was much, much better. They offered to pay me 10,000 dollars right away, then another 40,000 dollars when they make the movie, and also 1% of the net profits.

So that means now I would get 20,000 dollars right away, then *80,000* when they make the movie, plus 1.5% of the net profits.

Stefanie *did* always want to make the movie. She said, "I want this," right after I finished pitching the story on Skype. And she kept wanting it. The only reason she doesn't have it is that she won't let me write the screenplay.

Now she says I'll have "a significant consultation" with the screenwriter. How does that work? Does that person listen to all of my ideas, then take them and write the screenplay?

What if that person doesn't *like* my ideas? What if I don't like what they write? I already wrote a lot of the screenplay. Will they use what I wrote so far? If they do, will the credits say who wrote which parts?

There's a lot to think about. And we haven't even heard back from Hank Hollywood or Ashley yet. We can't decide right now. Dan Welch would say, "If Stefanie wants it as much as she says she does, she won't suddenly *stop* wanting it if we don't write back to her today."

chapter 24

I HATE PACKING!

I don't know why I can't just get over this and learn how to pack. But I can't. I don't want to think about what I'm going to wear the day after tomorrow. I have no idea. I hate bringing too many things, because it's too heavy, and I also hate being somewhere else and seeing clothes in my suitcase that I would never wear there in a million years.

Or if you don't bring enough, you just keep wearing the same thing, which I actually don't mind. But sometimes it bothers the people I'm with.

My mom used to pack for me, but she stopped a few years ago. I don't blame her. It's so strange to me that I know *exactly* what I want when I'm writing something or making a podcast, but I have *no* idea what I want when it comes to clothes. I put off packing until the morning of the trip. My mom won't even stay upstairs. "Sean, I love you, but I can't witness this." I just stand there and stare at my closet.

"Seany! Five minutes."

I start throwing things into the suitcase. It doesn't matter. If I need something I didn't bring, I can get it there. Thorny likes shopping. When Jakey and Rachael (my cousins) visit her, they always go to the mall. I'm not really a mall person—though now that I think of it, it might be a good place for a podcast.

My dad drove me to the airport in his van, which is always fun and much less embarrassing now that the slogan is gone.

"You're a brave man, Sean Rosen."

"What do you mean?"

"Getting on a plane by yourself. Getting into a car that my mother is driving. Spending three days alone with her."

"She isn't as annoying to me as she is to you. And I'm not as annoying to her as *you* are. Do you think she'll talk to me about Grandpa?"

"I can't even guess."

"Is it okay with you if I ask her about him?"

"Definitely. Just because *I* don't want to think about him doesn't mean *you* can't."

"Good."

"Seany, I know it sounds like I hate my parents."

"I understand, Dad."

"You do?"

"Well . . . if I found out you were robbing things from the houses you work in . . . I might not *hate* you, but I'd be really mad at you. You know . . . for embarrassing us. And for taking stuff you don't even need."

"Just for the record, I never even *thought* about taking anyone's stuff."

"I know. It was just an example."

"I'm supposed to remind you to text us when you land, and then when you get to Grandma's."

"No."

"No?"

"When you're on your honeymoon, you don't get texts from your son."

"I know. But your mom would feel better if . . ."

"Tell her I swear I'll call you if I need you."

"You sure?"

"Pretend I don't exist for three days."

"You crack me up. We'll do our best."

The flight was fun. Since I was flying by myself, the flight attendants kept checking on me and bringing me drinks and snacks. I took out my digital voice recorder and interviewed the people I was sitting next to. I'm not sure I'll ever use them in a podcast, but they have an interesting job.


```
ME:        How did you get started?
LADY:      For me, it was the family
           business. I started when I
           was three. I did it on
```

	stage for the first time when I was four.
MAN:	I never even *thought* about doing it until I met *her*.
LADY:	No. He isn't what you'd call a natural.
ME:	(to him) How did you learn?
MAN:	She taught me. One of her brothers helped too. You just have to practice. For hours and hours and hours.
LADY:	He isn't a natural, but he's got stick-to-itiveness.
ME:	He's got *what*?
LADY:	Stick-to-itiveness. He doesn't give up. He sticks to it until he gets it.
ME:	Oh.
MAN:	I was motivated. She was traveling all the time with the act, and I wanted to be with her. Plus, I was ready for a career change.

ME: What was your job then?

MAN: Long-distance trucking.

ME: Big change.

MAN: No kidding.

They're jugglers. They perform at senior complexes like the one Thorny lives in, but unfortunately they're not going to her complex this weekend. They wrote down where they're performing in case we want to come. I got them to juggle those little bags of peanuts. In their act, they juggle fire, but they don't let you do that on a plane.

I thought about telling them that *I'm* in show business too. There's a lot going on in my career, and sometimes not telling anyone about it feels lonely. Maybe the jugglers I met on a plane and will probably never see again are the perfect people.

But you never know who's going to post what you tell them. Some people never post (me), and some people post everything (Thorny, Brianna). I have no idea if these jugglers post or not. I don't want my parents and friends to find out about my career before I tell them myself.

The plane trip went really fast. Near the end, I took out my *Hollywood Reporter* to read. Maybe I was hoping the jugglers would ask me why I have it, and maybe I would tell them, or just tell them a little. But they either didn't see it, or they don't know the magazine. Now that I think about it, I've never seen an article in *The Hollywood Reporter* about juggling.

chapter 25

When I got off the plane, Thorny was waiting there. You're not supposed to be at the gate if you're not flying, but I guess she talked her way in.

"Look at you. You grew a foot."

"Actually, I already had both these feet."

"Funny boy. Seriously, you grew twelve inches."

"Since Jakey's bar mitzvah? Maybe one."

"Well, *I'm* shrinking, so it seems like more. C'mere, you."

She came toward me to give me one of those hugs. I took a step back.

"Grandma . . ."

"No more talking. I need a hug."

"But . . ."

"Get over here. Mmm-*mmm*."

Ouch. We'll definitely have to work on this.

Florida is nice and warm. Grandma drove us home from the airport. I wanted to go to her condo to change into shorts and use the bathroom, but she wanted to go to Publix (the gigantic food store) first.

"The restrooms there are very clean."

"You've been in the men's room?"

"As a matter of fact, yes. There was a line at the ladies' and I didn't want to wait. And trust me, they keep it so cold in that store you'll be *glad* you didn't change."

"What if I'm *not* glad?"

"You can complain about it the whole way home."

She was right. The men's room at Publix *is* very clean, and fortunately, no one's grandmother was in there. She was also right about the store being cold.

Thorny let me get whatever I wanted. I hate shopping for clothes, but it's fun being in food stores, especially when you travel. I like seeing products I've never seen before, even the store brands.

We walked up and down the aisles. Thorny doesn't really cook, but she loves eating and she loves when other people eat. I tried not to get *too* many things. For example, I don't think I should get more than one kind of cereal, because I'm only going to be here two mornings.

"Get what you want. Believe me, it won't go to waste. When you leave, you'll take it, I'll eat it, or I'll give it to someone."

It was fun, but I was glad to go outside. It's freezing in there. I was colder than the four kinds of ice cream we bought.

We got to her condo complex. It's called Paradise Valley. I'm not sure why. I mean, it's pretty nice. A bunch of buildings that all look the same. Palm trees, ponds with ducks, swimming pools, and lots of grass. Well, it *looks* like grass. Don't try walking on it barefoot. But there's no valley.

The first stop is always the clubhouse. You need a guest pass to be able to use the facilities. The clubhouse is a gigantic building filled with pool tables, card tables, Ping-Pong tables, a million other activities, and a giant auditorium.

We walked into the office.

"Sean! Welcome back! Look at you!"

Rosita has been working at the office since I first came to Paradise Valley, when I was very little. I never come more than once a year, but she always remembers me.

"Hola, Rosita."

"*¡Ah! ¿Hablas español ahora?*" ("You speak Spanish now?")

"*Sí.*" I used to take French, but there was this complicated situation with my French teacher, so I switched to Spanish. I like it.

"*¡Ven aquí y dame un abrazo!*"

I wasn't sure what she said. I've only been taking Spanish for a few months. Then she held her arms out. I went over and she gave me a hug. A nice normal hug. Thorny should take lessons from Rosita.

I got my pass, and we went to Thorny's condo.

"Come on, Sean. Let's go to the pool. Get your trunks on."

"My *trunks*?"

"Do not assume that the name *you* learned for something is the *correct* name."

That is so Thorny. I actually wrote it down, because I want Grandma in my screenplay to say that. I don't think I have to get permission from Thorny, because we're related.

There are pools all over Paradise Valley. We don't go to the one right near Thorny's condo anymore. I think she had a fight with someone. Probably not a hitting-each-other fight, but I'm not sure. She won't tell me. "It's not important. The walk will do you good."

Some of the people here go around on these big tricycles. They're just like the ones you rode when you were little, but they're grown-up size. I guess they're safer than bicycles. They look a little funny, but I still want to try one.

This isn't a regular vacation time, just a weekend, and the weekend didn't even start yet. My parents let me skip school today. Thank you, thank you, thank you. So I'm the only kid at the pool. Everyone here knows Thorny, and Thorny knows everyone.

"Everyone, this is my grandson Sean."

I didn't know what to do, so I smiled and waved to everyone.

"He promises not to splash you."

"I'll do my best."

Sometimes we come down here the same time as my cousins, and it actually is a little more fun to be in the pool with other kids. But there's also a better chance we'll splash someone. It's okay that my cousins aren't here. I'm not here for a vacation. I came to work. I got in the pool, and I listened to people's conversations to get ideas for the grandparents in my movie. Two ladies were standing in the water talking.

"Was it breakfast or continental?"

I swam over to them.

"Would you look at the head of hair on this one?" (She was talking about me.) "I would *kill* for that color. Literally. Kill. Would you please let me have your hair?"

"It depends. Who are you gonna kill?"

"He's clever too. Clever, and he has that hair. Life isn't fair."

"What did you mean when you said, 'breakfast or continental'?"

"Oh. Sometimes at a hotel, breakfast is included. They don't say it, but most of the time, they mean a continental breakfast, which is practically nothing. A danish and cup of coffee. To *me*, that is *not* breakfast."

"And juice." That was her friend.

"Juice? No. They give you the world's smallest glass of juice. It's not even a glass. It's a thimble."

"A what?"

"A thimble. An eye dropper. You don't know what I'm talking about. You're too young. A miniscule amount of juice. Less than a swallow. Half a sip. So if they say you get breakfast, find out in advance. Is it breakfast or continental?"

I got out of the pool and sat on a big chair reading *The Hollywood Reporter*. For about five seconds. Then Thorny tickled my foot.

"Get up. You've been sitting all day." I know what this means. She wants to play shuffleboard. She's really, really good at it.

"Let's go, Sean. A penny a point." She likes to play for money. I don't mind. I'm pretty good at shuffleboard too.

"Hah!" That was Thorny knocking my disk from ten to minus ten. I ended up owing her seventy-eight cents. And in case you were wondering, she isn't one of those grandmothers who bets and doesn't make you pay. And she never, ever lets you win.

We had dinner back at the condo. Later we were going to meet a few of her friends and go to a show at the clubhouse.

I told Thorny about the jugglers I met on the plane. I showed her their card.

"They're probably on the C or D circuit. We get better jugglers here."

"How do you know? You've never seen them juggle."

"And *you* have?"

"Not really, but—"

"That's one of the things you pay for down here. The quality of the entertainment."

"Is Paradise Valley very expensive?"

"Middle to upper middle. I'd call it a B."

"Have you been to nicer places?"

"I've been to more *expensive* places. I wouldn't call them nicer."

I wasn't planning to get into this so soon, but here goes.

"Dad said Grandpa made a lot of money."

"Grandpa made a lot of people miserable."

"Did he make *you* miserable?"

She looked at me for a minute. "Do you really want to do this?"

"Yeah. I mean, if it's okay."

"Okay. Sean, as you know, I think of myself as a smart woman."

"I think of you as a smart woman too."

"Thank you. But how smart could I be if I was living with a man who was stealing *millions* of dollars . . . from his *friends* . . . from *our* friends! . . . and have no idea it was happening? *That's* not smart. I still don't understand it."

"Why did he do it?"

"I don't know, Sean. He said it was like an addiction. Once he started, he couldn't stop. But why did he start? I don't know. To impress my family? Maybe. We had a little more money than they did. Because he felt cheated? Maybe. His mother died when he was fifteen.

"Whatever it was, it doesn't justify stealing. Stealing, lying . . . Sean, he *hurt* people. He made people's lives a lot worse. People he knew. People we were friends with. People who thought they had money for their old age and found out they didn't.

"And for what? To have a bigger number in a bank account that no one but him ever saw? We *didn't need* the *money*."

It sounded even worse than when my dad told me about it. "And you never knew?"

"I can't explain it. I can't forgive myself for it either, but no, I never knew. I knew he was a clever guy. He could have been making a good income legitimately. He did. For years. But then it changed, and I never knew.

"We didn't start living a different life. We were already comfortable. We didn't move into a mansion. We donated more money to causes I believe in, which made me feel very good. Until I realized it was money he was stealing from his clients. Our friends."

"How did you find out?"

"I found out when he got arrested. It was a total shock. And what was even more shocking was that he didn't even pretend he didn't do it. It was like he was relieved to get caught. He'd been living all alone with this secret for years, and it was finally over. At least for *him*.

"But for me, for your dad, for your aunt Sandy, and most of all, for his clients, the nightmare was just beginning. I apologized to each and every person he cheated. Even if they believed that I didn't know, which I doubt—*I* wouldn't have believed it—I couldn't make it right. We didn't have enough money to pay them back. It was a disaster."

"Did you visit him in prison?"

"Well . . . as you may know . . . as you *should* know, the criminal justice system in this country is horribly unfair. When a poor man steals a handbag, they lock him up and he stays locked up. When a man like your grandfather steals millions, he walks the streets for months or years until they finally have a trial.

"I lived at home with your grandfather after I knew. We went to your mother's graduation together, right before the trial. That was the day she and your father got married. Another big surprise."

"She told me."

"So by the time he finally got locked up, I didn't want to see him again, and he didn't want me to see him there. We both knew it was over."

Grandma got up and started putting things away.

"Before he got caught, did Grandpa *act* like a crook?"

"No! I'm telling you, he acted like every other guy who moves money around for a living. I wonder how many *other* crooks we don't know about. Anyway, that's why I moved to Florida. Nobody knows me here."

"Yes they do."

"Yeah, but they know me as *me*. Not as the crook's wife. Okay, enough. Let's go see a show."

chapter 26

Thorny's couch is comfortable. When my parents
come, we stay in a motel, so I never knew that. We
had some breakfast (not continental), then I started
thinking about checking Dan Welch's email.

Thorny doesn't really like anyone using her
computer (I know how she feels), but I didn't
bring mine, and I want to see if we heard
anything from Ashley or Hank Hollywood.
I offered to borrow one of her neighbors' trikes
(that's what they call those giant tricycles), and
use one of the computers at the clubhouse. "Don't
be ridiculous. Use mine. Just don't download
anything or click on a link."

Facebook was on the screen. Now I know how

celebrities feel when they read what other people say about them.

Sean and I discussed the meaning of life, then we went to a concert at the clubhouse by "The Israeli Adele." She *was* Israeli, but she's no Adele.

"The meaning of life"? I don't know what she means by that, but even though it was hard to hear those things about my grandfather, I'm glad she told me.

Thorny's right about the Israeli Adele. The show was pretty bad. She kept asking everyone to clap along to the songs. This is never a good idea. A whole room full of people can never clap together and sound good, especially to a song they never heard before that's in Hebrew.

I didn't want to read any more posts about me, so I went to Dan Welch's inbox. He has two new emails.

Okay. Now I'm nervous. I shouldn't have looked. I'm going to be with Thorny for the rest of the day, starting in about ten minutes. What would be worse? Wondering what's in those emails the whole day? Or looking at them now and thinking about them all day but not talking about them?

I think I have to open them now.

To: Dan Welch Management
From: Dan Welch

Dan, Dan, Management Man,

When oppertunity knocks, you gotta anser the door, buddy! I dont want it to slam in our face. I know you said youd handel it, but this Hollywood person came to Me, and if I dont get back to them soon, Im afraid Ill hurt my credabilitry. Yours and Seans too.

Talk to me, Dan Welch.
Dan Welch

Sorry, Collectibles. You should have forwarded the whole email from Ashley right away. You shouldn't have made us wait.

But now that I think about it, Dan Welch and I are making Stefanie wait. I mean, while we see if Ashley or Hank Hollywood decides to bid on the movie. But also so she'll want it even more. Is what Collectibles did any worse?

I actually think it is. Collectibles talks like he's part of our team, but he isn't really. I'm the writer. *A Week with Your Grandparents* is something I made up myself. Dan Welch is my manager, and he actually *earns* his 15% of everything I make ($0.00 so far). Collectibles is just the guy Ashley accidentally wrote to when she was looking for me.

The other email is from someone I never heard of. I like the email address. I wonder if it's another Hollywood studio. That would make four.

To: Dan Welch
From: icanseethetopofyourhead

Hi, Sean. It's Ethan. Hope you're having Fun in Florida. Something weird happened. A girl came up to me in school and said, "You're friends with Sean Rosen, right?" I never saw her before, but there are lots of people in school I never saw before. I didn't answer. Then she said, "You work with him on his podcasts, right?" I still didn't say anything, but I didn't walk away either, so she probably took that as a yes. Then she said, "Is he good with computers?" I didn't know what to say. You are, but so is everyone, more or less. I didn't answer. Then she said, "What other things are you guys working on?" This girl is really pretty, Sean. <u>Really</u> pretty. Like so pretty she expected me to tell her everything she wants to know. I was afraid I might, so I started to leave. She followed me and said, "Has he ever told you any of his ideas?" I started walking faster, because you <u>did</u> tell me one of your ideas, and I was afraid she was going to use her powers to get me to tell her. It's a good thing I take big steps. See you Monday.

Okay. I officially wish I didn't open that email. Who was that girl? How did she know that Ethan is my friend? And that he works on my podcasts?

Ethan thinks she was asking about *A Week with Your Grandparents*, because that was the idea I told him. I actually think she was trying to find out what my big idea is. The only one who even knows I *have* a big idea is Hank Hollywood. How did he get a pretty girl in my school to help him?

Ethan doesn't have my regular email address, so he got Dan Welch's from my website. I once asked him to be Dan Welch, so he knows there isn't a real one and that Dan Welch's email goes to me.

"You ready, Sean?"

Not really, but since I can't do anything about this until Monday, I might as well have fun with Thorny and do what I came here to do.

We went to Butterfly Kingdom, which is like a theme park with no rides. The theme is butterflies. They have a lot of them. And I guess they're always there, or they wouldn't be able to make you pay so much to get in.

Maybe they stick whatever butterflies like to eat on all the trees and bushes. Like if you had a place called Teenager Kingdom, you'd have free Cokes and Snickers and donuts everywhere, so there would always be teenagers when people came to see them.

Butterfly Kingdom is nice. Quiet. Like the opposite of a video game.

Then we had lunch, then we went to the movies.

There was a movie playing at the clubhouse at Paradise Valley, but we decided to go out to a movie instead.

We found a movie we both wanted to see, and Thorny bought our tickets.

"One senior and one child."

"Umm . . . actually, I'm not a child anymore. I'm thirteen."

Thorny looked at me for a second, then said, "Sorry. One senior and one adult."

We went in, found our theater, and sat down. We were early, and I didn't want popcorn because I was still full from lunch.

"I know I look twelve and under."

"I forgot for a minute. Maybe because you didn't have a bar mitzvah."

"I can pay for my ticket."

"No."

"Are you mad that I told them?"

"Not at all."

"I want to be in the movie business someday." (Like NOW.) "Movies are expensive to make. The people who make them have to get paid. Everyone should pay the right amount for their movie tickets."

"You're right. What kind of movies will you make?"

"I'm glad you asked that question. I'm writing one now, and I need your help."

I told her the story of *A Week with Your Grandparents*.

"Grandma in my movie thinks it's a bad idea for people to visit the past of someone they know."

"Well, *I* wouldn't do it."

"Why not?"

"The past is past. If I can't change it, why should I go through it again?"

"Maybe you missed something the first time. You know how when you talk about something you did with a friend, you don't remember it the same way? You can use the time machine to find out what really happened.

"Or if you want to see something you weren't able to see. Like if I wanted to go to my parents' wedding. I actually *don't* want to do that, but I could."

She thought about it some more.

"I don't know, Sean. If I went back in time, I might see that I was only *pretending* not to know what was going on with your grandfather."

"Is that what you think you did?"

"Sometimes I think that. Because I just can't believe I didn't know."

"It sounds like Grandpa was really good at fooling people. Maybe if you went back, you'd see why you didn't know. Maybe it was impossible to know."

The lights went down, and the coming attractions started. Grandma grabbed my hand and squeezed it really hard. It hurt a little, but less than a hug.

It was a very good trip to Florida. My parents picked me up at the airport. It was like the last part of their honeymoon, before we all went home. They looked happy. It wasn't like going to their wedding in the time machine, but after talking about them with Thorny and seeing them together at the airport, I could picture them as boyfriend and girlfriend. Not just my parents.

chapter 27

Monday morning my first class is history. Morning is a good time to have history, because there's less of a chance I'll fall asleep. I got there just as the bell rang, so I didn't get a chance to talk to Ethan.

I looked at him, and he looked at me, but unfortunately Mr. Knapp started talking. How can anyone make a world war—like a gigantic people-killing-people-from-other-countries-all-over-the-world war—*this* boring?

I don't like passing notes in class. Well, I like it, but I don't like getting caught, which is usually what happens. But the combination of

Mr. Knapp's voice and me dying to find out, made me write this note to Ethan.

Did you see that girl today?

I didn't actually pass it to him. I just wrote it big in my notebook and held it up. He's not looking at me. I cleared my throat really quietly. A few other kids turned and looked at me, but Ethan didn't. I put the note away.

I was deciding whether or not to drop a pen on the floor when he finally looked at me. I quickly held up the note again. He looked at it, and then he gave me a look like, "What??"

I took the note down and looked at it. Ethan can't read it. I'm not surprised. Not everyone is good at reading bad handwriting. I am. But I get a lot of practice reading my own.

This time I tried all capital letters.

DID U SEE THAT GIRL TODAY?

Now he can read it, and he shook his head no.

He didn't shake his head in an obvious way, but Ethan has a really big head, and he usually sits still (not like me), so when he shakes his head, people notice.

"Ethan, are you saying that England was *not* one of our allies in the war?"

"No."

"Then what *are* you saying?"

"Nothing."

"My mistake. Mr. Rosen, is something amusing?"

"Sean, you're tan."

It was Brianna. We were in the hall after history, and I was just about to ask Ethan about that girl.

"I forgot to wear sunscreen to Butterfly Kingdom."

"You look good."

"Thanks. You do too." She actually had a little too much makeup on.

"Thanks. *Le Bistro* today."

"Right."

Le Bistro is the show that Mademoiselle Fou, the French teacher, puts on each year. I was the host last year, but I thought the show was really bad (Mademoiselle Fou can't sing, but she sings constantly in the show). When I wouldn't be in it this year, she started giving me bad grades. That was what made me switch to Spanish. Brianna plays a French fashion model in *Le Bistro*.

"Sean, I know you said you're not coming, but you should."

"I would, if I could see *you* without seeing the rest of it."

"I don't think it's as bad as last year."

"You wouldn't even know. You're always offstage changing."

"That's true. Buzz is coming."

"Really?" Bad idea. Buzz doesn't speak French, and he knows the difference between good music and bad music. "Brianna, Ethan, you know each other, right?"

"Hi."

"Hi."

Call the *Guinness Book of World Records*. Those

were the two unfriendliest "Hi"s ever.

Brianna said, "Gotta run."

Ethan was looking up and down the hallway. He can see everything from up there.

"I don't see that girl."

"I know how to find her. Meet me in the Publication Room, seventh period."

This was Ethan's first time in the Publication Room. Only the yearbook kids and the school newspaper kids use it. Luckily, no one else is here. I opened the computer file of yearbook pictures.

"What grade do you think she's in?"

"Has to be eighth. She's not like any of the girls in our classes."

We looked at every eighth-grade girl. "She's not here. Trust me, I remember her."

Then we tried the seventh graders. He didn't see her there either.

I opened the page of sixth graders. "Don't bother. This girl *can't* be in sixth grade."

"Like *you* can't be in seventh grade?"

We looked. She isn't.

"This girl knows things about you, Sean."

"But how did she know that you work on the podcasts?"

He thought for a few seconds. "If someone went to your website when your address was still there, they would know where you live. You talk about the library podcast on your website. There's only one library in this town. They call the library. Everyone there knows you. 'Oh, yeah, Sean Rosen. He was here with that big kid.'"

"There are *other* big kids."

"Not from up here, there aren't."

"Come with me to the principal's office."

ME:	**Trish, do you know Ethan?**
TRISH:	**Of course I do. I know everyone.**
ME:	**And everything.**
TRISH:	**True.**
ME:	**Good. We came to the right place. We're looking for**

the name of a new girl in school. Ethan, tell Trish what she looks like.

ETHAN: (embarrassed) Very pretty. *Very* pretty.

TRISH: I need a little more.

SEAN: She started here after yearbook pictures were taken.

TRISH: There's only one student who's *that* new. And I wouldn't call him pretty.

ME: Could a girl who didn't go here get into the school?

TRISH: (to Ethan) Did she look like a student?

ETHAN: Yeah. The world's prettiest student.

TRISH: If she walked in with a big group of students, Ms. Crincoli might not notice her. So Ethan . . .

sounds like someone has a crush on someone.

The door opened, and I couldn't believe who walked in. Brianna's dad. Standing a foot away from me. He doesn't see me. I'm sort of hiding behind Ethan.

"Who do I talk to around here?"

Trish said, "Possibly me. What can I help you with?"

"This is a two-thousand-dollar suit. The lady at the front door is telling me I have to wear *this*"—it's the blue visitor's sticker—"and it has go right *on* my suit. Are you prepared to pay my dry cleaning bill?"

"I'm not, actually, but why don't you hand it to me?"

"My suit?"

"No. The sticker."

He looked at her for a minute, then he handed it to her. She opened a drawer in her desk and pulled out a clear plastic holder. She slid the sticker inside and handed it back to Brianna's dad.

"If you'll just put that in your jacket pocket . . ."

He put it into one of the side pockets on the bottom.

"No. The chest pocket. Where people can see it."

He gave her another look and then moved it.

"Thanks. Makes everyone feel a little safer. I'm sure you understand."

I finally said something. "Hi, Mr. _____."

"Oh. It's you."

"Sean."

"Right. This is Ethan." Neither of them said anything, so I kept going. "Are you here for *Le Bistro*?"

"Whatever it's called."

"*Le Bistro*. You want me to show you where the auditorium is?"

"I can find it."

He turned around and left.

ME: Is two thousand dollars a
           lot for a suit?
TRISH: I'll tell you *this* much.
           It looks a heck of a lot
           better than my husband's
           ninety-nine dollar suit.

chapter 28

Ethan went to *Le Bistro*. I went back to the Publication Room. I wasn't completely sure I put everything away. I did. I was also sort of hoping Mr. Hollander would be here. I feel a little bad not telling Trish the truth about that girl or why people might be asking about me.

Trish is my friend, and she does a lot of nice things for me. Why don't I just tell her about my career? I'm not ashamed of it. I'm not breaking any school rules. I thought if I saw Mr. Hollander right after not telling Trish, maybe I would just tell *him* the truth. He's another person I think of as a friend. But if I'm going to tell these people at school, why don't I just tell my parents, who are like my *best* friends?

At the beginning, when I was trying to get people in Hollywood to listen to my ideas, I didn't tell anyone I knew because I thought they would tell me I was crazy to even try. But now people in Hollywood are writing to me, chatting with me, and trying to buy my movie. I think they're even sending people to my town to find out about me. Maybe it would be good to have some friendly grown-ups (besides Dan Welch) help me figure it out.

So if it's Hank Hollywood who got someone to call the school and then got a pretty girl to *come* to the school, what is he trying to do? If he wants to know about my idea, why doesn't he just ask me what it is? He knows how to reach me. Why is he sneaking around?

Oh my God. I just figured it out. He's trying to steal my idea. He figured out that it's worth a lot of money, and instead of asking me what it is and having to share the money with me, he's going to find out what the idea is and use it and not pay me. He could probably get away with that.

Maybe I *should* tell someone, because then I

would have a witness. Now that I think about it, I haven't even written the idea down anywhere. If Hank Hollywood's company suddenly started using it, there would be no way to show that *I* had the idea first.

This is hard. But I can't think about it anymore right now. I have to go to Baxter's house so Mrs. Dahlin can tell me what to do when they're away.

On my way out of school, I passed the auditorium. I thought about going in for a second to see a little of *Le Bistro*, but then I heard Mademoiselle Fou singing, and it sounded just as bad as last year. Right then, the door to the auditorium opened and Buzz walked out.

"Sean. That is the worst ____ I ever saw in my life."

"That's why I'm not in there."

"Why didn't you warn me, man?"

"I thought about texting you, but if she found out . . ."

"I know. I know. This whole thing . . . her . . . being back in this school . . . I'm going crazy. I gotta get out." He ran out the door.

Buzz used to go to school here, but he was having trouble in most of his classes, so his parents moved him to a private school. Then they moved him to a *different* private school, the one he goes to now. He likes this one. He gets to play guitar in his classes, and they go on a lot of trips.

I wonder if Brianna knows he bailed on *Le Bistro*.

I better get moving too.

"We're leaving at some ungodly hour in the morning, so you're in charge of Baxter all day tomorrow. We get back the next night kinda late. So you'll walk him and feed him twice that day, and we'll do his third walk when we get home."

"Sounds good."

"Here's his food. You mix a can of this . . . with a cup of this."

"What size cup?"

The minute I said it, I knew it was a stupid question. She's holding a measuring cup.

"Just use this. Measure out one cup. What time will you come over in the morning?"

"Before school."

"When's that? No kids, remember?"

I actually forgot. I guess you don't have to know when school starts if you don't have any kids and you don't work at a school.

"Guess."

"Guess?"

"Guess what time school starts."

"Really? I don't know. Nine?"

"I wish. Try seven fifty-five."

"I never knew that."

"So I guess I'll be here at seven."

"We'll be gone by then. You still want to do this?"

"Definitely. Is that okay, Baxter? Seven tomorrow morning? Too early?"

"If it means food, you can show up at three in the morning, wake him from a deep sleep, and he'll be in love with you the second he hears this cabinet door open. Okay, these are his treats."

"Can he have as many treats as he wants?"

"No, Sean. Unless you want to be in charge of treats for the rest of his life. Let's say six treats a day. Less if he's bad."

"Bad?"

"He's never really *bad*."

"Sounds like he *sometimes* is."

"I just mean . . . like if he chews up my dish towel."

"Has he done that?"

"Not for a while."

"When was the last time?"

"Two years ago."

"What else does he do when he's bad?"

"Oh, you know. The usual. Climbing on other dogs and not getting off when you say no."

"What do I do if that happens and I say no and he doesn't stop?"

"Just yank the leash. Here's our cell numbers. Bob never has his on, so call mine if you need us. Even if you just have a question. Don't worry about interrupting. We're visiting my in-laws. They're exhausting. A phone call from you will get me out of the room for a little while. Like a little break. But that's really not your job. What I'm saying is, don't hesitate to call me."

"Okay."

"Here's the fifty dollars. Are you sure that's enough?"

"Unless he's a bad dog. Just kidding, Baxter. You're gonna be very, very good, right?"

He wagged his tail and licked my hand.

Walking home from the Dahlins, I got a text from Brianna.

Did u see Buzz? He wasn't there after the show and he's not answering my texts.

Uh-oh. I'm not going to answer.

My dad is in the driveway, getting ready to put a sink into his van.

"Shawnee Mission, Kansas!"

He calls me that sometimes. It's an actual place. He's never been there, but he says it because Shawnee sounds like his nickname for me.

"You'll never guess who called me today."

I didn't say anything.

"Aren't you gonna guess?"

"If you tell me I'm never gonna guess, why bother?"

"Good point. Your grandmother. My mother."

They almost never talk on the phone. They figured out that whenever they do, they fight, so my mom usually handles the phone calls with Thorny.

"She called to tell me that somehow, in spite of *me* being your dad and *her* being your grandma, you're turning out okay."

"Is that what she actually said?"

"Something like that."

"You want a hand with that?"

"I got it. Thanks."

Oh, no. Another text from Brianna.

Where is he?????

I better text back.

Don't know. Sorry.

chapter 29

The doorbell rang. I ran downstairs. It was a tall man with dark hair. He was wearing sunglasses, even though it wasn't sunny out.

"Hi." That was me.

"Are you Sean Rosen?"

"Actually . . . yeah."

He stuck out his hand, like to shake hands. I didn't know what to do, so I shook his hand.

"Hank Hollywood. Glad to finally meet you. Mind if I come in?" He didn't wait for me to answer. He walked right in.

"We have a lot to talk about, Sean."

We *do* have a lot to talk about, but I wasn't expecting to do it right now, right here in my own house. My parents still don't know about any of this.

"You look nervous, Sean. Would you prefer I talk business with Dan Welch?"

The second he said "Dan Welch," I heard a terrible loud sound. Like the Truth Police were coming to arrest me.

Hank Hollywood just stood there waiting, but I couldn't talk. I didn't know what to say, and I couldn't think because of that horrible sound.

That horrible sound. My alarm clock. I woke up and turned it off. My clock says 6:02. What a scary dream.

Is that what Hank Hollywood looks like? I don't even know. I Googled him, but I didn't look at pictures of him. I want to do it right now, but I don't have time. I have a lot to do this morning.

When I got to the kitchen, my mom was there having coffee, dressed in her nurse clothes.

"Hey, early bird. Are you gonna get the worm?"

"I hope not."

"It's an expression. The early bird gets the worm. Birds eat worms. There's a limited supply.

So the birds that get up early get the worms."

"Very interesting. I have to go feed and walk Baxter. Hmmm. I wonder which one you do first."

"Mrs. Dahlin didn't say?"

"No. I could call and ask her, but I think I'll just Google it." And make myself not look up Hank Hollywood.

I made my lunch, then ate some cereal. It was actually one of the ones I bought with Thorny that she told me to take home.

"My little boy's growing up."

"Finally."

"Flying to Florida by yourself, taking on new responsibilities . . ."

She's talking about Baxter. What will she say when she finds out about Dan Welch and the bidding war for my movie?

"I should get going."

"Google. Dog info."

"Oh, right. Thanks." I ran upstairs.

"Baxter! Good morning. Have you been up long?"

It's funny to ask a dog a question. You wait for

an answer, even though you know you're not going to get one.

"Okay, Baxter. It's walk first, then eat. Everyone says so. How many plastic bags do you think I'll need? Two? Three? Twenty-three? Just kidding, just kidding."

Do dogs ever get jokes?

I remembered to lock the Dahlins' door, so nobody will rob them while Baxter and I are walking. I don't think our neighborhood has ever gotten robbed, but you don't want to be the first.

I was glad I walked Baxter before this, because I know what to expect. It's actually nice to be out this early in the morning. I only needed one plastic bag, which I put in the garbage in the park.

There were a few other dogs in the park. Baxter didn't climb on top of any of them, so I gave him a treat.

We got back to the Dahlins, and first I filled up Baxter's water dish. He was a little thirsty after our walk. Then I mixed up his food, which he started eating the second I put it on the floor.

"Okay, Baxter. I would love to stay and play, but

I have to go to school. Have a good day. See you this afternoon."

I gave him a treat before I left. He would probably appreciate it more in a few hours as a snack. You know, when he isn't already eating his regular food. But I decided not to bother suggesting that to him, because the treat was gone as soon as Baxter saw it.

Every time I go to the cafeteria for lunch, I remember why I never go to the cafeteria for lunch. Noisy, smelly, and all those kids. You're trapped in rooms all morning with kids. You don't need any more of it.

I wish I could go say hi to Baxter, but we aren't allowed to leave school during lunch. Since I'm stuck here, and I want to talk to Ethan, the cafeteria is a good place. We actually have more privacy here than almost anywhere, because he has his table, and no one ever sits with him except me.

On my way to Ethan's table, I saw Brianna and she saw me. I waved, and she didn't wave back. She just made a sad face, like the human version of ☹.

I guess Buzz hasn't texted her back yet.

I sat down with Ethan and opened my lunch.

"How was *Le Bistro*?"

He didn't say anything. He just held his nose.

"I know. You haven't seen that girl again, have you?"

He shook his head.

"Ethan, you have a phone, right?"

"Sort of." He reached into his pocket and pulled out the exact same old-fashioned flip phone that I have. "My brother had a cool phone."

"You mean, until the . . ."

"No. Even after the crash. It's in a box. We have a big stack of boxes with his stuff."

"Would your parents let you use it?"

"I doubt it. I don't want to ask."

Ethan gave me his phone number, and I gave him mine. He's turning into a good friend, and if Hank Hollywood actually *is* trying to steal my idea, and if that girl shows up again, we have to be able to communicate quickly.

As soon as I finished eating, I left. I was walking toward phys ed when I heard:

"Sean Rosen . . . please report to the principal's office."

Here we go again. Too bad we can't use our phones in school. Then they could text you to come to the principal's office instead of announcing it to every single person in the whole school.

Trish was waiting for me. "Sean, someone just called here about you. Mr. Parsons is going to tell you about it. It's not that woman who called that day. We checked it out, and it's a real thing."

I must have looked nervous.

"Don't worry. It's good."

I have no idea what she's talking about.

"Okay." I walked into Mr. Parsons' office.

"So, Sean, how come I never knew about these podcasts?"

I like Mr. Parsons, but I hate questions like that. "I don't know."

"They're very clever."

"Thanks. Did Trish tell you about them?"

"No. She knew about them?"

"I only told her like a week ago."

"How long have you been doing them?"

"I started last year."

"They're very clever."

"Thanks. Was there something else?"

"Yes. We got a call from *Teen Doers*."

"From *what*?"

"*Teen Doers*. It's a magazine. They're legit. Trish checked it out. They want to interview you."

"They do?"

"Yes. About your podcasts."

"Really?"

"Yes. Your podcasts aren't a secret or anything, are they?"

"No."

"Then why didn't I know about them?"

"I don't know. . . . I wasn't sure I wanted people at school to know. You never know what people are going to make fun of."

"They're good, Sean. What would anyone make fun of?"

"How I talk, how I sing, my songs, my questions, the people I interview—"

"Okay, okay. You're probably right. Well, *Teen Doers* is an online magazine, and since *I* never heard of it and *you* never heard of it, chances are it doesn't have a big readership at this school. So your secret might be safe."

"Unless someone Googles me."

"Oh, right. Well, I'll leave it up to you. If you want to be interviewed, you can do it after school right here. I'll have the reporter call my number, and you can talk to him in my office. We'll have to clear this with your parents, of course. Do *they* know about your podcasts?"

"Yes. Definitely."

"Good. So what do you think?"

"I'm usually the one doing the interviewing. It might be fun to be on the other side."

"Okay, good. An article about you could be helpful . . . you know, when you're applying to colleges. Good. See you here after school."

I got to phys ed late. They were in the middle of a game of something. Mr. Obester saw me walk in.

"Rosen, you're late. Go to the principal's office."

"I just came from there."

Javier came over. "Coach, this is the truth. We all hear the message."

"We all *heard* the message." (That was me.)

Then Javier imitated the message. "'Sean Rosen, report to the principal's office.'"

"Back to the game, Javier." Then Mr. Obester turned to me. "We lost that track meet."

"Sorry."

"By just a few points."

"I'm really sorry." I don't know if I should have said this, but I did. "I would have run in the race if you let me."

"Get changed."

He put me on Doug's team. Now that Doug knows I can't help the band get famous, he isn't pretending to be nice to me anymore. I thought it was good that I was on his team so he wouldn't be attacking me (I swear, I don't know what game this is), but being on his team is even worse.

He keeps passing the ball to me when I don't expect it, and when I drop it and the other team picks it up, he says, "You suck, Rosen." I guess

Doug doesn't mind losing the game if he can make it look like it's my fault.

After phys ed finally ended, I walked to my last class with Javier.

"Sean, are you on trouble?"

"*In* trouble. No."

"Good. Want to come over after school?"

"I can't. I have this thing. Then this other thing."

"Okay, my friend. Good luck with your things."

Probably *everyone* thinks I'm in trouble. I went into the boys' room and texted Ethan.

No news on mystery girl, but some magazine, Teen Doers (??) wants to interview me about the podcast. If you want to come, it's in Mr. Parsons' office after school.

He texted right back.

Good luck.

I actually didn't think he'd come. A second later, I got a text from Brianna.

I need you after school.

There's too much going on.

Sorry. Can't today.

chapter 30

It actually *is* interesting being the person getting interviewed. You have no idea what they're going to ask you, so you can't really prepare. I thought about looking at my podcasts, but I don't have to. I know every word and every picture of every podcast. That's what happens when you work on something for hours and hours that only lasts a minute.

So I'm just sitting here in Mr. Parsons' office waiting for the phone to ring. He's here too, but he's going to leave when the reporter calls. Meanwhile, he's staring at his computer screen. Students, teachers, the principal . . . everyone looks exactly the same when they're looking at their computer.

Trish stuck her head in.

"Sean, you want some water?"

"No thanks."

"Are you nervous?"

"I don't know why, but yeah."

"You'll be great. I shouldn't be watching your podcast. Now I'm dying for a donut."

The phone rang. Mr. Parsons, Trish, and I all looked at each other.

Mr. Parsons said, "It's showtime." Then he picked up the phone. "Hello." He listened for a second. "Oh, hi, Ben. Yeah, Sean is right here. Hold on a sec." Then he covered the phone and said, "Sean, I can put the phone on speaker if you want."

"No. I mean yes!"

I quickly pulled out my digital voice recorder and hit RECORD.

Mr. Parsons and Trish left the room and shut the door. Then I heard the interviewer's voice through the speaker.

BEN: Are you there, Sean?

ME: I'm here.

BEN: Hi. My name is Ben Patel,
        and I'm the editor of *Teen
        Doers*. Do you know our
        magazine?

ME: Well . . . I've seen it. I
        mean, I saw it today.

BEN: We write about
        entrepreneurial kids.

ME: About what?

BEN: Kids who are entrepreneurs,
        who start their own
        businesses. Kids who are
        doers, not just watchers.

ME: Okay.

BEN: So, your podcasts are
        pretty cool.

ME: Thanks.

BEN: How did you get started
        with that?

ME: Well . . . there's this

donut place I like to go to after school. I would sit there and eat my donut, and just . . . I don't know . . . listen to people's conversations. All kinds of people go there—kids, grown-ups, rich people, poor people, people from all different countries—so it's always interesting. My MP3 player has a microphone built in, so one day while I was sitting there, I hit RECORD. When I got home, I listened to it. I liked it. You felt like you were actually *at* the donut place. Then the next time I went, I asked someone if I could interview them.

BEN: A stranger?

ME: Yeah.

BEN: About donuts?

ME: Exactly. It was fun. *I* had
           fun, and the lady I talked
           to had fun. People *like*
           being interviewed. Then I
           went back a few more times.
           I taught myself how to edit
           on my laptop, and I put
           together a little donut
           show.

BEN: And *that's* the donut
           podcast on your website?

ME: No. I liked what I had,
           but it was a little hard to
           hear. This was right around
           Hanukah and Christmas—
           we celebrate both in my
           family—so I asked my
           parents for a digital voice
           recorder. They got me a
           good one, so now when
           I record interviews, they

	sound a lot better. Then I started taking pictures, so you can *see* the person I'm talking to.
BEN:	But you never show us anyone's face.
ME:	I know. It's partly so people will let me take their picture. More people say yes if they know you won't see their face. Plus, I like that you have to imagine what people look like from hearing their voices and only seeing parts of them.
BEN:	You're a songwriter, too.
ME:	Sort of. I knew I wanted music in the podcasts. I thought I would just use songs that I like. Like famous songs. But I found out you have to get

permission and you also
have to pay someone a lot
of money. It's just easier
to write the songs myself.
Plus, I couldn't find any
songs about donuts. I *had*
to write one.

BEN: I like it.

ME: Thanks. It's fun to do, but
it takes me a long time,
because I don't play any
instruments.

BEN: Do you make any money doing
this?

ME: No. I actually *spend* money.
You know, on donuts and
things.

BEN: Would you like to do this
professionally?

ME: Make podcasts?

BEN: Yeah.

ME: I don't know. Maybe.

BEN: Why wouldn't you?

ME: I like doing it the way I do it. If someone was paying me, I'd have to do it the way they want me to.

BEN: What *would* you like to do professionally?

ME: Something in entertainment.

BEN: Like be a performer?

ME: No. You heard me sing. I'm not really a performer.

BEN: Then what would you do?

ME: I don't know. Make movies. Make TV shows. Maybe games.

BEN: Do you have any specific ideas?

ME: Actually . . . can you hold on a minute?

BEN: Sure.

I walked out of Mr. Parsons's office and closed the door. Only Trish was there.

"How'd it go?"

"It's still going. But I want to stop."

"Why?"

"He's asking me some questions I don't want to answer."

"Is he still on the phone?"

"Yeah."

"I'll tell him you're done."

"Is that okay?"

"Definitely. How was the rest of it?"

"Good. He sounded really interested in my podcasts."

"I'm sure he is."

"What will you tell him?"

"I'll say you had to leave, and that you said you enjoyed talking to him."

"That sounds really good."

"Sean, I do this all day long."

"Thanks."

chapter 31

What is going on here? Does this Ben guy work for Hank Hollywood too? Is any of this actually happening, or am I just going crazy? That's what I was thinking as I walked out of school.

"Finally." Brianna was standing there.

"Hi."

"We're going to Buzz's."

"Now?"

"Yes."

"I can't right now."

"Yes you can."

"He still hasn't answered your text?"

"*Texts.*"

"How many?"

She pulled out her phone and looked at it for a little while. "37."

"Wow."

If I texted someone 37 times and they didn't answer, I definitely would *not* want to go to their house and try to talk to them, but I'm not Brianna. She grabbed my arm and started walking toward Buzz's.

"What are you gonna do when we get there?"

"Ask him what's going on."

"I don't want to be there for that."

"Too bad, Sean. *You* got me into this."

"No I didn't!"

"He's *your* friend, right?"

"Yeah, but . . ."

"We're going there."

She started walking faster.

"Let go of my arm."

She did. I stopped walking.

"Brianna . . . are you sure you want to do this?"

"I'm sure I don't want to wait one more minute to see if some boy is *ever* going to text me back."

"Do you want *me* to find out?"

"Oh! Look who's finally ready to help a friend."

"I'm here with you, aren't I?"

"Only because I dragged you. Is there something you know that you haven't told me?"

"Well, actually . . ."

"I am *so* mad at you right now."

"It isn't much. Buzz . . . hated *Le Bistro*."

"Duh. Anyone with a brain hated *Le Bistro*."

"But you made him come see it."

"Because I was *in* it."

"I know, but did you say, 'The show is really bad, but I want you to see *me*'?"

"No."

"Then he probably thinks you thought it was good."

She thought about that.

"He said he wanted to come."

"Because you made him think it was going to be good. Anyway, even if he wanted to *come*, he didn't want to *stay*."

"He *left*?"

"Yes. You don't know. You never see the show. It's bad. Really bad."

"My dad liked it."

"Buzz isn't your dad. Seriously . . . did you really think he'd like it?"

"Seriously . . . I just wanted him to see me in it."

I stopped walking and just looked at her for a second.

"What do you like about Buzz?"

"What do *you* like about him?"

"I asked you first." I said that in a little-kid voice. We started walking again, but not as fast. I thought about it. Then I answered the question. "He's my friend. We've been friends since we were little. We see each other like once a month. We play Wii baseball. I don't know. I like him. I like his music."

"*I* like his music. Sort of."

"Sort of? What else do you like?"

"I like the way we look together." She showed me a picture of her and Buzz on her phone.

"When was that?"

"That first night at band practice."

"What else?"

"I like kissing him."

"Oh." I didn't know what to say.

"Did you ever kiss anyone, Sean?"

"Actually . . . no."

"Well, it's nice."

"Good. So . . . what are you going to say to him when we get there?"

"I don't know. That I'm mad at him for ignoring me."

"Show me the last text you sent him."

WHAT IS WRONG WITH YOU???

"I think he already knows you're mad at him. Do you just want to know if it's over?"

She didn't say anything. This time she stopped walking. "Why does he spell like that?"

I laughed. "He just does."

"He's not being clever or creative, is he?"

"No."

She looked at me for a second, then said, "I could show you what it's like."

"What *what's* like?"

"Kissing someone."

"Really?"

"Yeah."

"That's nice of you, but . . ."

"You don't want to."

"No. It's just . . ."

"There's someone you like."

"No. There isn't. I just . . . really have to pee."

She laughed. I laughed.

"Okay, Sean. You can go home."

"What are you gonna do?"

"Go home."

"You're not going to Buzz's?"

"No. I don't feel like playing Wii baseball. Whatever that is. I'm going to stop texting him too."

"Really?"

"Really. Thanks."

chapter 32

I hurried home. Should I have kissed Brianna? I wasn't expecting her to say that. I really do have to pee. And I don't think I want my first kiss to be a friend doing me a favor. Especially after she said she liked kissing Buzz. What if I'm a bad kisser? How do you even know?

My phone beeped. It's from Ethan.

How was the interview?

I tried texting back while I walked, but I'm not really good at that, so I stopped walking.

Good, then not good. Tell you later.

I got home, and my dad was there.

"Hi. Bathroom."

He laughed as I ran up the stairs.

Okay, I feel better now.

I want to call Ethan to tell him about the interview, but I'm going to check Dan Welch's email first.

Finally! She wrote back.

To: Dan Welch Management
From: Ashley _____

Dear Dan,

Sorry for the delay getting back to you. I wanted to have my ducks in a row first. Unlike Stefanie and that horrible business affairs department at my previous employer, we don't believe in trying to screw the artists we're going to be working closely with for the next few years (and hopefully, the rest of their careers). A refreshing change, wouldn't you agree?

Here's what we're thinking:
— $25,000 for a two-year option on *A Week with Your Grandparents*
— $85,000 production bonus when the movie gets

made (in addition to the option money)

— 2% of the net profits

—as soon as the deal is signed, two business-class tickets to Los Angeles and first-class hotel accommodations for Sean and a parent, to begin work on the project

—my personal guarantee that Sean will be heard, and that I will work tirelessly to make sure *A Week with Your Grandparents* is the movie he wants it to be.

Dan, I'm just realizing that I don't even know where Sean lives. Where will we be flying him in from? Doesn't matter. Timbuktu? No problem. He's going to love being out here. We'll make sure he sees the sights, and maybe he'll even meet a star or two.

Give me the word, and I'll send the paperwork. Do it soon, though. I can't wait to get started, and the sooner we start, the sooner the world will know Kris and Chloe and their unexpectedly cool grandparents.

Best,
Ashley

Hmmm. She spelled Chris's name wrong. I guess she only heard me say it on Skype. We'll have to tell her. I wonder if I get to choose which stars I'll meet when I go to Los Angeles.

Everything she offered us is more than Stefanie.

	ASHLEY	STEFANIE
Money I get now	$25,000	$20,000
When they make the movie	$85,000	$80,000
Net profits	2%	1.5%
Other	Trip to LA	

That's interesting that everything is just a little bit more. It's like Ashley knew what Stefanie offered.

Does Ashley have a spy at her old studio? Maybe Stefanie's assistant, Brad, is telling Ashley things. I never knew Hollywood was like this. I actually don't know if it is, or if I'm just imagining it. Like, is Ben Patel from *Teen Doers* actually a spy for Hank Hollywood?

I looked up *Teen Doers* online before my interview, and it's a real site. Maybe Ben Patel really *was* just asking the next question, not helping Hank Hollywood steal my big idea.

Just as I opened my phone to call Ethan, there was a sound from my laptop. It's Stefanie, starting a chat.

STEFANIE: Hi Dan.

What should I do? I wanted a bidding war, and now I have one. But I still don't know if Hank Hollywood is going to bid. Oh well. Here goes.

DAN: Hi Stefanie. How's Marisa?

STEFANIE: She's fine. It's my in-laws who are driving me crazy. Hovering grandparents. I'm tolerating it now in exchange for free babysitting later.

DAN: Sean just visited his grandmother. Research for the movie.

STEFANIE: Yes, the movie. When can we start?

DAN: Sorry I didn't get back to you. Sean was away, and we've actually gotten a higher bid.

STEFANIE: From that snake Ashley? Dan, friend to friend, her bid is meaningless. Sean will *only* see the option

money. She is not capable of getting a green light. With her, the movie will *not* get made.

Is that true? How does she know?

STEFANIE: We'll match whatever she offered, though *I* know and *you* know that in this case, the intangibles are worth more than money.

I looked up intangibles. "Not tangible." Great. Now I have to look up tangible. "Something you can touch." What is she talking about? Can you touch a trip to Los Angeles?

DAN: You said that Sean would have a significant consultation with the screenwriter. What do you mean?
STEFANIE: Sean will be part of the team. It's *his* idea. He'll meet with me and the screenwriter before he or she starts writing, and Sean will tell us every single thought and idea he has about the characters and the story.
DAN: Then after he or she writes the screenplay, will Sean be able to read it and make changes?

STEFANIE: Dan, you know this. NO ONE has script approval. Academy Award-winning screenwriters don't control their screenplays. It's the law of the land.

DAN: I'm going to have a hard time convincing Sean.

STEFANIE: I know it's a bitter pill for writers and would-be writers to swallow.

No one said anything for a little while.

STEFANIE: I'm going to promise you something, and if anyone ever asks, I'm going to say that I never said this. But I promise that when the screenplay is finished, I will secretly slip you a copy to show to Sean. I will personally review each and every note he may have about the screenplay. Here's where you'll both have to trust me and my years of experience and my track record in this business. I will take his notes and use my judgment about what makes sense for the project, and I will communicate that to the right person.

Hmmm.

STEFANIE: No one, no one, *no one* will offer you more input than that. If they do, they're lying.

DAN: I'll tell him.

STEFANIE: Do more than that, Dan. Tell him the facts of life. Tell him I'm not in the habit of going this far out on a limb, and tell him that I'm not going to stay here forever. I love him, I love his project, but soon I will move on. I'll be very sad, but I'll move on.

DAN: Okay. Thanks, Stefanie.

STEFANIE: You know how when you break up with someone, all of your friends finally tell you the truth about them? Well, that's what happened when Ashley left. If you want to talk to some other people about her, let me know, and I'll put you in touch. It'll make your hair curl.

Is that true?

STEFANIE: OMG, Dan . . . do you even *have* hair? I keep forgetting we never met.

DAN: I do have hair.

STEFANIE: Phew. I have to run to a meeting. Let's do this, Dan.

DAN: Talk to you soon.

It's so weird. When I finished reading Ashley's

email, I was sure I was going to work with her. Now I'm sure I'm going to work with Stefanie. Why wouldn't I? She'll match whatever Ashley offered. I guess that includes the trip to Los Angeles. But how about meeting stars?

I read Ashley's email again. She never said anything about me writing the screenplay. According to Stefanie, *no one* will let me. Might as well find out.

To: Ashley _____
From: Dan Welch Management

Dear Ashley,

Good to hear from you. I know Sean would want me to tell you that his character's name is Chris, not Kris.

I have to run to a meeting, but before I take your offer to Sean, I want to make sure that Sean will be writing the screenplay for *A Week with Your Grandparents*.

Best,
Dan Welch

chapter 33

When I came downstairs, my dad was in the kitchen standing on a ladder, changing a lightbulb.

"I can't wait for you to grow a few more inches, Seany."

"You would trust me on a ladder holding a lightbulb?"

"Yes. I'll train you, then I'll trust you."

I opened the refrigerator. I'm not even hungry. But sometimes you don't know that until you're looking at food.

"Dad . . . how do you know who to trust?"

"In business or in life?"

"Is it different?"

"Is it different . . ." He stopped working for a minute to think about this. "Well . . . with anyone, you listen to what they say . . . and then you see what they do. But you may not know for a while if you can trust them or not. They either screw up or they don't."

"When you say screw up, you mean like Grandpa?"

"No. That was worse than screwing up. That was out-and-out stealing. No. I'm talking about when someone does something selfish, something he knows is gonna hurt you . . . then he pretends he didn't know it was gonna hurt you."

"Give me an example."

"Okay, someone I know, a guy I did a few small jobs for, made me think I had this really big job. A new building. He picked my brain for hours and hours—like three separate times. He got me to tell him how I'd do it, what products I'd use, how I'd work with the electrician, everything. Then he used all of my ideas, but got another plumber do the work."

"Why?"

"I don't know. He thought he'd save a few bucks. I don't think he did. Anyway, I trusted this guy who was just using me to get information."

"What did you do?"

"There was nothing I *could* do. Except never work with him again. But it still hurts. I trusted him. He acted like we were friends. He still acts like we're friends. It reminded me that business is business. Believe me, it would have been much worse if a *real* friend did something like that to me."

I thought for a minute. Did *I* ever do that to a friend? Did I do that by pretending to Buzz about Dave Motts? I hope not. Maybe I stopped just in time.

Then I thought about Stefanie and Ashley.

"Do a lot of people in business pretend to be your friend?"

"Yeah. They do. I'd say about . . . half of them."

"What do the other ones do?"

"They're just themselves. Some are nice. Some are weird. Some don't *want* to be your friend. That's fine with me. Let's just get the work done and go home to our real friends."

"Interesting."

"Seany . . . I'm just gonna assume that when you want to talk to me about something . . . you know . . . something that's going on with you . . . you'll just *do* it, right? I mean, you don't want me to . . . drag stuff out of you. Do you?"

I had to think about that. Sometimes I think I actually *do*.

"No. That's Mom's job."

"And she's so damn good at it."

"Too good."

"She's working tonight. How about an early dinner at the diner?"

"Like now?" Suddenly I'm hungry.

"Yeah." He got down off the ladder. "Let's go. You can tell me about the movie you're writing. Or not."

"Did Mom tell you?"

"No. Grandma did. She said she can't stop thinking about it."

"Really?"

"Yup."

"I didn't know that. That's good."

We both like this diner. They know us there. Dad had a grilled Swiss cheese with bacon and tomato and a cup of soup, and I had a fried fish sandwich. We shared an order of fries. I had a chocolate shake.

My mom called while we were there. She asked me about the interview. She was the one the school called to get permission.

I told my dad I'd rather have him read the screenplay when I finish it than just tell him the story. He said okay.

After we ate, Dad was going to meet his friend Ray to go bowling. He asked if I wanted to come, but he knew I didn't. He already has his bowling ball in the van, so he's just going to drop me at home. We drove past the Dahlins' house, and oh my God! Oh my God! OH MY GOD!!!

I totally forgot about Baxter.

chapter 34

I jumped out of the van. I didn't say good-bye to my dad. I couldn't talk. I sort of waved.

I can't believe I did this. How could I do this? My first day taking care of Baxter, and I forgot all about him. He hasn't been walked or fed since seven this morning. That's almost twelve hours!

What does he do when he can't get outside? Pee on the floor? Poop on the rug? Look for an open window?

I ran into our house and up the stairs to my room. I fell on the stairs. Maybe I'm hurt, but who cares. Poor Baxter. I got the key to the Dahlins' house out of my backpack and kept running.

Is he okay? Did he eat furniture because he ran out of food? I am such an idiot. I thought about all the things I was doing when I should have been with Baxter. Talking about my podcast to some spy. Listening to Brianna complain about Buzz. Pretending I'm a talent manager chatting with a vice president. Talking to my dad about trusting people. *I'm* the one you can't trust.

I'm sorry, Baxter. I'm sorry.

I got to the house. There's a light on. Did I leave it on? Maybe they left it on for Baxter. What am I gonna find when I open this door? I'm scared.

I opened the front door. When I did that this morning, Baxter ran over and jumped on me. But now, nothing. I stood there and looked around. No pee. No poop. No dog.

I'm so scared. I don't even know what I'm scared of. But I'm too scared to talk. I'm scared that if I yell "Baxter!" he'll be so mad at me that he'll run over and do something like . . . I don't even know what. Bite me? No. I don't think so. But if I had to pee for hours and hours and it was your fault, maybe I *would* want to bite you. Or pee right in front of you here on the rug.

So I didn't call him. I sort of tiptoed through the house. There's no light on in the kitchen, but with the living room light on, you can see in there a little bit. Oh, no. The kitchen floor is wet. What is it? It's probably pee. Oh, Baxter. It's my fault you had to pee in the kitchen. But where are you?

I'm a few steps closer now. I see a wire. Like an electrical wire. It's lying in the puddle. This is bad. Wires are not supposed to be in puddles.

I'm scared. I take one more step. Wait. That's Baxter's leg. He's lying on the floor. Right next to the puddle. He's not moving.

Oh my God. Oh my God. I electrocuted Baxter. I can't breathe.

I make myself take another step. It's him. He's lying there. He's not moving. I killed Baxter. I started crying. What should I do? Should I call 911? It's too late for 911.

He's dead. And I did it. I can't look at him. I went back to the front door. I just stood there. I don't know what to do. I took out my phone and called Ethan. He answered right away.

"Hi, Sean. . . . Are you there? . . . Hello?"

I hadn't said a word the whole time I was at the Dahlins'. It took me a few seconds to be able to talk.

"Ethan . . . I did something terrible." I was still sort of crying.

"Where are you?"

"Right around the corner from my house. In the blue house with the fence."

"I'll be right there."

Ethan didn't even ask me what I did. He's coming. I don't know what he can do, but he's coming. What is wrong with me?

God, can't you punish *me* and not Baxter? *He* didn't do anything wrong. He was such a great person. I mean dog.

I'm going back in there. He's dead, but still. I don't want him to be alone.

I walked back into the kitchen. It was still dark in there.

"Baxter . . . I'm sorry, boy. I'm so sorry. You were the best dog ever. How am I gonna tell the Dahlins?"

Wait.

I think he moved.

No. I'm imagining it. I turned on the light.

"Baxter . . . are you . . . not dead?"

He picked his head up. He's ALIVE! Thank you, God.

But wait! He's right next to the puddle and the wire. "Baxter! Don't move!"

I guess he was sleeping before, and now he's awake. He's moving.

"Stay away from the puddle!"

Does he even know what a puddle is? I ran to the other side of the kitchen, away from the puddle.

"Baxter! This way! Come here. Come to me."

He ran over to me. "Good boy. Baxter, I'm so sorry."

He stopped listening. He's starting to go to the back door, which is on the other side of the puddle.

"No! No, Baxter!" He has to pee. He wants to go out.

There's a knock at the front door. I hope it's Ethan.

"Come in!"

I hear the door open. "Sean?"

"We're back here. Ethan, call Baxter."

"What's his number?"

"No! No! He's a dog! Just call his name!"

"Baxter! Come here, Baxter!"

Baxter ran toward the front door. I want to get his leash, but it's on the other side of the puddle, near the back door. I can't reach it.

"Just hold him. I'll be right there."

Ethan has him. Baxter is shaking. He looks like he's going to explode. I take his collar, and we go outside. He wants to run, but I'm holding on to his collar with both hands. Ethan is looking at me like I'm crazy. So is Baxter.

Baxter lifts his leg and starts peeing. And peeing and peeing and peeing.

"Did you ever hear of a leash?" It's not Ethan. I look up. It's Mr. Bentley, who lives a few houses away. He's standing in the street looking at us.

"Thanks, Mr. Bentley. Next time I'll try that." He walked away. Baxter kept peeing.

He finally stopped. I waited to see if he wanted to poop too, but either he doesn't have to or he *can't* with me holding his collar. We went back inside.

"Ethan, can you go close the door to the kitchen?"

I sat down with Baxter and apologized about ten more times. Then, when Ethan came back, I explained what happened.

"I was sure I electrocuted him. I still think I did."

"No. We couldn't have touched him if he was electrified."

"But there was a wire in a puddle of whatever that was."

"It's water. Come here. I'll show you."

All three of us looked in the kitchen.

Ethan pointed. "See? He knocked over his water dish trying to get the back door open. And that's just an extension cord. That can get wet. What you don't want is a *bare* wire in the water." Ethan unplugged the extension cord and used paper towels to wipe up the floor. "Because if Baxter was standing in the water and he chewed on that wire, that would have been it."

"I'm surprised he *didn't* chew on that wire,

because I also forgot to *feed* him for twelve hours."

Baxter must know the word "feed," because he went right over to the cabinet where his food is. I gave him two treats while I got his real food ready.

"Ethan . . . should we take him to the vet? Just to make sure he's okay?"

We stood there and watched Baxter eat.

"Nah. He's fine. We'll take him for a walk when he's done eating."

He was done in about twenty seconds. "Should I give him more? He missed a meal."

"Maybe after the walk."

"That's right. Walk first, then eat."

chapter 35

The three of us walked to the park. No one said anything for a while. That's normal for Ethan and Baxter. I think I was still trying to believe that Baxter is really alive. That was the worst I ever felt in my life.

Baxter's walking along the exact same way he always does. Looking around, sniffing things. I don't know how he does it. He walks down this street every single day, but he always acts like he's seeing it for the first time.

Finally Ethan said something. "I looked up *Teen Doers*."

"Ugh. I didn't think of Baxter even *once* during

that whole interview. I am a bad person."

"You're just not used to taking care of a dog."

"I'm not used to taking care of anything. Not even myself."

What if I really *am* a bad person?

"You do a lot of things. Maybe you don't have time for a dog right now."

"Still . . . you'd think I could take care of Baxter for a day and a half without killing him."

"You didn't kill him."

"Right."

"Nice try, though."

"Shut up."

"So . . . *Teen Doers*. It's an online magazine about kids who start businesses and charities. They should just call it GettingIntoCollege.com."

"Sean Rosen. I read about him in *Teen Doers* . . . but I hear he kills dogs. Should we accept him . . . or reject him?"

"The magazine is owned by _____." That's Hank Hollywood's company.

"No it isn't."

"Yes it is."

"Wow."

"What?"

"It's complicated."

Ethan waited to see if I was going to say anything else. We got to the park. Baxter pooped. I'm glad. He *is* all right.

"Ethan, I feel bad not telling you things."

He didn't say anything.

"I swear it's not because I don't trust you. Because I *do*."

He didn't say anything. We just kept walking.

"This sounds like an excuse, even to *me* . . . but I don't want to get you in trouble. You know, if *I* get in trouble. You know . . . for what I'm doing."

He finally said something. "Sean, when you're ready to tell me something, you just will. That's okay."

"Thanks."

"But you don't have to worry about *me*. I'm not afraid of getting in trouble."

I thought about that. "Well . . . you already know way more than anyone else. You're the only person who doesn't work in Hollywood and isn't my grandmother who knows the story of *A Week with Your Grandparents*."

"That's the name of it?"

"I thought I told you."

"No. You just told me the story."

"What do you think?"

"It's . . . it's not . . . it's just not as interesting as the movie is."

"I agree. What should the name be?"

"I don't know. Did you change the story much?"

I had to think about that. "No. The story hasn't really changed. But there are lots of new things. New characters. New places they go to in the past. You get to know everyone a lot better. So the basic story is the same, but now it's a lot more interesting."

"Cool. It was already good. Well, whenever you're ready to know what the average American teenager thinks, I'm ready to read it or hear it or whatever."

"Average?"

"Joke. Is it really gonna be a movie?"

"It *might* be. And not 'might' like 'Anything is possible' or 'Never say never.' But 'might' like it really *might*. But I really don't know."

We're almost back at the house.

"Do you think I should I tell the Dahlins?"

"The *what*?"

"The Dahlins. Baxter's family."

"Tell them *what*?"

"That I almost starved and electrocuted their dog."

We both looked at Baxter.

"Nah. He's fine."

"Okay."

"Set an alarm on your phone so you don't forget again. Even these dorky phones have alarms."

"Good idea."

After Ethan left, I went home and got my homework and brought it back to the Dahlins'. Baxter sat and watched me work.

I apologized a few more times, but I actually think he isn't mad at me. If he did the same thing to me, *I* would be mad. But he's a dog. In my song about dogs in my podcast there's a line, "Whatever you do, he always forgives you." I don't know why, but it's true.

chapter 36

Wednesday morning when I went to walk Baxter, it was like nothing happened. He's fine, and we had a very nice walk. We didn't talk about what happened yesterday. Sometimes when you apologize too much, you don't sound sorry anymore, just annoying.

I fed him, then I looked around the kitchen. It looks normal, except I'm not sure where the Dahlins usually have that extension cord.

"Okay, Baxter. Enjoy your breakfast. I'll see you after school. I promise."

The day in school was okay. I wasn't called to the principal's office. Nothing unusual happened, which was totally fine with me.

At the end of the day, all the seventh graders had to watch a bus-safety video for our trip to Pine Tree Wilderness Retreat this weekend. I took a lot of notes.

Afterward, Javier said, "Amigo, are you nervous about the bus?"

"No. I was writing down ideas for a funny bus-safety podcast."

"*Siempre estás pensando.*" ("You are always thinking.")

"*Es verdad.*" ("It's true.") Sometimes I think it would be easier to not have so many ideas, but I guess I'll never know, because I just do.

The minute school was over, my Baxter alarm went off. Thanks, Ethan.

On my way to the Dahlins', I got a text from Buzz.

We

He wants to play Wii baseball.

Can't today. Tomorrow?

Oka

That's probably a yes.

When Baxter and I got back from our walk, the Dahlins' car was in the driveway. They weren't supposed to be back until late tonight. I'm a little sad.

"Hi, boys!" That's Mrs. Dahlin saying hi to Baxter and me. He looks happy to see her. Not like relieved happy. Just happy. "How'd it go?"

Part of me wanted to tell her how it actually went. But a bigger part of me wants to do this again sometime. I'm sure I won't make such a big stupid mistake again.

"We had a good time together. Right, Baxter?" He jumped up and licked me, so I guess it was okay to say that.

"My in-laws were driving me nuts, so I talked Bob into coming back early. Fortunately for me, he hates to drive at night. I mean, *today* it was fortunate. Some nights it's a pain."

"Can I feed him? Baxter, I mean. Not Mr. Dahlin."

"Sure. But if you gave him too many treats, I'm gonna be able to tell."

"I didn't. I swear."

I said good-bye to Baxter. I offered to give Mrs. Dahlin some of the fifty dollars back because she came home early. She wouldn't take it.

I still feel bad that I forgot about Baxter yesterday, and getting paid for doing a bad job makes it even worse.

When I got home, I looked up the address of the animal shelter in my town. I'm going to give them the money. I thought about keeping half of it, because I did my job right most of the time, but I think for this kind of job you shouldn't get paid unless you do it right *all* of the time.

Okay. The Dahlins are home. Baxter is fine. I can get back to work on my career.

Hank Hollywood is officially trying to steal my big idea. Here are the facts:

1. He figured out where I live and had someone call my school to check.

2. He sent a pretty girl to my school to find out what the idea is.

3. He got a magazine his company owns to do an interview with me to trick me into telling them my idea.

He could have just written back to Dan Welch and set up a meeting with me and *asked* me what my idea is. But if he asks me and I tell him, he has to pay me. *That's* why he keeps trying to find out other ways. I think.

But WHY??? You are super rich. You make fifty million dollars a year. Your company makes billions of dollars. Every year. Why do you have to steal ideas from thirteen-year-olds? I don't expect you to give me billions of dollars. Whatever you pay me, you and your company will still have plenty left.

Now I'm glad I haven't told anyone my big idea. Because even though I'm good at keeping a secret, I don't want anyone else, like my parents, to have Hank Hollywood, the shark who scares all the other sharks, coming after them.

I Googled him again, but this time I went to images. He doesn't look anything like the Hank Hollywood in my dream. That one was tall and had dark hair. The real one is short and a little strange looking. It's weird. He looks *exactly* the same in every picture. It's like there's one look he puts on his face whenever he sees a camera. Or maybe he always has that look on his face, even when there's no camera.

While I was online, I decided to look up Ashley. She's on Facebook. I already know what she looks like from our Skype meeting. I didn't find anything else about her. There's a picture of her at a party, but that's about it. Maybe Stefanie is right that Ashley won't be able to get my movie made.

Stefanie isn't on Facebook.

Brianna changed her Relationship Status. She's not "In a Relationship" anymore. I thought she might change it to "It's Complicated," but I don't think it really *is* complicated. She's "Single."

I wonder if Dan Welch should write to Hank Hollywood again. What would he say? "We know what you're up to. It ain't gonna work, Mr. Hollywood." Dan Welch wouldn't say "ain't." *Collectibles* Dan Welch would.

What I'd really like to do is get Hank Hollywood to bid on *A Week with Your Grandparents*. It's getting better and better with two bidders, so if there are three bidders, maybe I can get even *more* money and *more* net profit points, and an extra business-class ticket to Los Angeles, so both of my parents can come with me.

I can't stop seeing Baxter on the floor next to the water and the wire. I actually *did* think he was dead. When he moved, it was like the happiest second of my life.

What if he *did* chew that extension cord while he was standing in the water? That could have happened. Dogs probably don't know not to do that. Would he definitely die as soon as his teeth got to the bare wire? Maybe he would just get a really terrible shock, and he'd open his mouth and let go of the wire and not die.

Maybe all that electricity going into your body would give you some kind of super power. Not like being able to fly or spin super-strong spider webs. Maybe something smaller. Like the power to read minds.

But if your dog could suddenly read your mind, how would you know? He can't talk. Hmmm.

Okay, so a kid comes home after forgetting about the dog, and finds him lying near the puddle with the wire in it. The kid . . . let's call him . . . Luke. Luke thinks his dog, whose name is . . . Mojo, is dead.

But then Mojo gets up and starts walking around. Luke is relieved, of course, but he doesn't know what to do next. Should he take Mojo to the vet? Luke's parents are both out. They just got this dog after Luke begged them for years.

He decides to call his friend Noah. He might know something. But Luke can't find his backpack, where his phone is. He looks all over for it. Suddenly Mojo walks over, carrying the backpack in his mouth. Luke can't believe it.

"Good boy, Mojo. How did you know I was looking for that?"

Luke starts to call Noah, but then he remembers that Mojo hasn't been outside in a while. He turns and Mojo is standing at the front door, holding his leash in his mouth.

"Mojo, did you just read my mind again?"

Mojo just looks at Luke. He can't talk.

Luke takes Mojo outside. After Mojo is done, Luke decides to try an experiment. He sits across from Mojo. He doesn't say anything. But what he's thinking is, "Okay, Mojo, touch my right leg."

Mojo just sits there looking at Luke.

"Oh. Of course. You're a dog. You don't know left and right. Okay." (Luke points.) "*This* is my left leg, and *this* is my right. Left. Right. Got it? Good."

Luke stops talking and just starts thinking, "Mojo, touch my left leg. My *left* leg."

Mojo walks over, lifts up his paw, and touches Luke's left leg.

"Amazing! Good boy! Nice work." He gives Mojo a treat.

Then Luke looks at Mojo and thinks, "Mojo . . . show me where you sleep."

Mojo turns around and walks to the family room, where his doggie bed is.

Luke calls Noah and tells him to come over. Luke wants to see if Mojo can hear all human thoughts or just Luke's.

Noah gets there, and he and Luke go into another room, so Mojo can't hear. Luke tells Noah what's going on. Then they get Mojo, and as an experiment, Noah thinks, "Mojo . . . take a drink of water."

Mojo walks to the kitchen and slurp, slurp, slurp.

It's incredible! A dog that can read human thoughts. At first, it's just a game, but then Mojo's new power leads him and Luke (and sometimes Noah) to all kinds of adventures. Luke's parents don't know. No one does except Luke and Noah.

This could be a really cool TV show. It would be funny most of the time, but also scary and exciting sometimes.

Luke and Noah discover that Mojo can only read *human* thoughts, not the thoughts of other dogs. This sometimes gets them into trouble.

And since Mojo can't talk, sometimes he knows things that he wants to tell Luke, but can't figure out how. When that happens, Mojo has to get Luke's attention, then have him ask yes-or-no questions, which Mojo answers by touching

Luke's left leg or his right leg.

It would be fun if the audience can hear the human thoughts that Mojo hears. Then *we* know more than Luke does. So sometimes we and Mojo know that the boys are in danger, but *they* don't know. We watch them figure it out by guessing and asking yes-and-no questions.

So it's sort of a comedy-adventure, with a little bit of a game thrown in. I like it.

What should it be called?

Luke and Mojo.

No.

I Know What You're Thinking.

Not bad. Wait. I have it.

Electro-Pup.

Thanks, Baxter.

chapter 37

To: Hank Hollywood
From: Dan Welch Management

Dear Hank,

We haven't heard from you for a while. (We actually *never* heard from him, just his assistant and all his spies.) I wanted to say hello, and I thought you might want to be the first to know about the latest Sean Rosen project.

It's a comedy series about Luke, a 13-year-old boy who begs his parents for a dog. They finally get him one, an adorable pooch named Mojo. The first day home, Luke accidentally partially electrocutes Mojo. The dog survives, and now he can hear human thoughts, which only Luke and his friend Noah know about. Since Mojo can't talk, Luke and Noah have to guess what Mojo is trying to tell them, using yes-or-no questions. The boys and the dog get into adventures and they also get into trouble. It's called *Electro-Pup*.

You're the only one we're showing this to, so if we don't hear from you in a week, we'll assume you're not interested.

Best,
Dan

I went to Buzz's after school, and as usual, we played Wii baseball. Buzz always wins, and he always wins by a lot. I decided that today it was at least going to be close.

Unfortunately, me deciding that didn't really change anything. When it was 27-2, we decided to take a break.

First we went to the Great Hall of Snacks. Whoever picks what's in this giant freezer really knows what they're doing. I had a pizza bagel, then a frozen Snickers. Delicious.

Then we went outside and stood on the side of Buzz's house. Buzz had a cigarette. I never saw him smoke before. No one said anything for a minute. Then he did.

"So, uh . . . sorry."

"For what?"

"You know . . . Brianna."

"Oh. Don't be sorry. Well, I mean not to *me*. I mean, I don't know what you did. If you did anything. Actually, what are you sorry for?"

"Oh. Her and I . . . you know . . . we're not . . ."

"Oh. I know. Don't be sorry about *that*."

"You sure?"

"Definitely. I actually never thought you two . . . anyway, that's between you and her. I mean *you're* my friend and *she's* my friend, and . . . to tell you the truth, it's easier for me this way.

"Good."

"Good. Buzz . . ."

"Yeah?"

"You look really stupid smoking."

"I do?"

"Yeah. You look like you're trying really hard to look cool. But actually . . . you don't."

"Are you sure?"

"If my phone had video, I'd show you."

He put out the cigarette. I felt a little bad.

"I thought you'd want me to tell you."

"I do. I guess. So . . . there's this song."

"Yeah?" He didn't say anything. "A song you *wrote*?"

"Yeah."

"What's it about?"

"It's like a . . . song about a girl."

"Oh. When did you write it?"

"Like a few weeks ago."

"Oh. I'm afraid to ask you this . . . but is the girl's *name* part of the song?"

"Yeah."

"Okay. And you like the song?"

"Yeah. A lot."

I had to think about this. "Well, if Brianna hears the song, she'll either want to get back together with you or she'll want to kill you."

"Yeah. That's what I'm afraid of. Both those things."

"In the song . . . does anything rhyme with her name?"

Buzz sort of sang through the song in his head, but out loud a little. "No."

"Then just change the name."

"Really?"

"Yeah."

"To what?"

"Anything that has the same number of syllables and the same rhythm as Brianna. Like Maria . . . Diana . . . Melinda . . . Jordana . . . Chiara . . . Mikayla . . . Alyssa . . . Sophia . . ."

"Stop. Sophia."

He sang through the song again in his head, but when he came to the name, I could hear him say "Sophia."

"It works."

"Good. When Brianna hears it, she might still want to get back together with you or else kill this girl Sophia, but . . ."

"I know. But now I can at least sing the song."

chapter 38

We were at the table after dinner, looking at the list of what to pack for the seventh-grade trip to the wilderness.

DAD:	We can buy you a sleeping bag.
ME:	For one night? That's a waste of money.
MOM:	How much does a sleeping bag cost?

No one said anything. None of us can even guess, because none of us ever even *thought* about buying a sleeping bag.

ME: Ethan's got two.

DAD: Let *him* have the big one.

MOM: Was the other one his
          brother's?

ME: I don't know.

MOM: I'm glad you don't care,
          Sean. Some people are funny
          about things like that.

ME: He didn't die in the
          sleeping bag. He might not
          have even used it. Ethan
          and his Uncle Neil are
          the only ones in his family
          who like camping.

DAD: Is his uncle one of the
          chaperones?

ME: No. He doesn't live around
          here. I still can't believe
          I'm doing this.

MOM: It's only one night.

ME: Then why don't *you* go and
          say you're *me*.

MOM: They won't believe me. I'm not cranky enough.

ME: Just don't do anything fun this weekend. I mean anything *I* would think is fun.

MOM: We'll do our best not to have fun. At least packing will be easy. They gave you a list.

ME: This list is confusing. They say to bring *hiking* shoes, but they also say not to bring *new* shoes. How many kids have *old* hiking shoes?

DAD: I bet Ethan does.

MOM: I bet Brianna doesn't.

ME: You know Brianna?

MOM: *Le Bistro* last year. She was the Paris model. And I drove you to her mansion.

ME:	Right.
MOM:	Anyway, you can wear your running shoes.
ME:	You're not mad at me for not being on the track team, are you?
MOM:	No.
DAD:	No.
ME:	Good. (looking at the list) If we're only there for two days, why do they say to bring three pairs of underwear?
DAD:	In case a bear attacks you.
MOM:	Jack . . . .
ME:	Why would . . . Oh. Right.

Saturday morning the alarm went off super early. It took me a minute to remember that the trip is today. Fortunately, I made myself pack last night.

It actually wasn't that hard. There are more

things on that list that we *can't* bring than things we *have* to bring. We're not allowed to bring any electronic devices, except our phones, which the chaperones will be holding for us.

Even cameras are not allowed. The year that got the seventh-grade trip cancelled for three years, some boys snuck over to the girls' cabin and took some inappropriate pictures.

I have one of the school cameras, so I can take pictures for the yearbook. They have it set up so I can't send any of the pictures anywhere (just in case they're inappropriate—they won't be).

The buses were in the school parking lot. Ethan was waiting for me with both sleeping bags. We're assigned to the same bus. Before my phone was collected I got a text from Brianna.

See you up there.

I texted back.

Which bus r u on?

No bus. I get nauseous on buses. My dad is driving me up. You want a ride?

With her dad? Is he a chaperone??

No thanks.

"I'll take that." I looked up. Mademoiselle Fou! *She's* one of the chaperones. "Remind me, Gaston (that was my French name when I was still in her class). What's your English name?"

She knows. "Sean Rosen." She wrote my name on an envelope and put my phone in it. She didn't ask Ethan for his phone. She probably thinks he's someone's dad. She walked away.

"If she sings at the campfire tonight, I'll . . . I'll. . . "

"Set yourself on fire?"

"I'll want to, but I probably won't."

Ethan and I played cards for a little while, then I walked around the bus taking pictures of everyone. Mademoiselle Fou made me wait until she checked her makeup. It doesn't matter. She's not going to be in the layout.

The bus driver is funny. I wish they let me bring my digital voice recorder. I would definitely interview him. He made some good faces in the pictures I took. He *is* going to be in the layout.

Ethan brought a book with pictures of plants and insects and other things you might find in the woods. He really does like nature. The pictures are pretty. It made me a little excited to be there.

As we got closer to the place, you could tell we were in the wilderness. Ethan showed me which trees are pine trees. And here we are. Pine Tree Wilderness Retreat.

chapter 39

Thank goodness Ethan and I are in the same cabin, because if I walked into this cabin by myself, I would walk right out, find Mademoiselle Fou, get my phone back, text Brianna and beg her to ask her dad to drive me home.

It's like a log cabin with ten cots in it. That's all. No sink. No bathroom. One light in the ceiling. Pine Tree Wilderness Prison. Help!

Ethan said, "Don't worry. By the time we get back here tonight, we'll be so tired, we'll fall right to sleep and it won't matter where we are."

The bathroom is a separate building. You walk down a path to get to it. No wonder we had to bring a flashlight. I'm actually glad the bathrooms aren't in these little cabins. It would be too embarrassing.

We put our sleeping bags on our cots, then everyone went to a big wooden building they call the mess hall for lunch, which was soup and sandwiches. I looked around the big room for Brianna. I didn't see her.

The mess hall (which is actually very neat) has a lot of tables. Looking around, I see that everyone is sitting almost exactly where they sit in the cafeteria, with the exact same kids. That includes Ethan and me, who are at a table by ourselves in the corner.

It's also as noisy as the school cafeteria, but it just got quieter. I turned around to see why. It's Brianna. She's walking across the mess hall wearing a pink . . . I don't know what you call it . . . it's almost like a spacesuit. She has pink shoes, too. She's carrying a little black box. She sees me and waves. Now she's sitting with her usual group of girls.

She looks happy. I guess she really *is* over Buzz.

I'm glad she hasn't heard his new song, "Sophia."

I wonder which other teachers and parents are here. I look around the room and don't see Brianna's dad, but there's Mr. Obester. There's the assistant principal.

"Hi Sean. Hi." Brianna came over and sat down with us. I'm glad she finally said hello to Ethan, too. He might have nodded to her, but I couldn't tell for sure.

"You look very. . . pink."

"I know. I couldn't resist."

"What is that box?"

She opened it. "Oh, just a little bento box. We passed a sushi place on the way, and I brought it just in case." She pointed to our sandwiches. "Good thing I did, right?"

"How's your cabin?"

"My what?"

"Your cabin. The girls are in cabins too, right?"

"Oh. Probably. I'm staying at a cute little B&B."

"B&B?"

"Bed and breakfast."

"Hi, Brianna." It was Doug. He sat down next

to Brianna. He didn't say anything to Ethan or me.

Brianna said, "Do I know you?"

"Doug. From Taxadurmee."

"What's that?"

"You know. The band. Buzz."

Brianna got up. "I have to get back to my friends." She left.

Doug sat there for a second, then must have realized he was sitting a table with only Ethan and me, because he got up so fast his chair fell over. He didn't pick it up.

———

After lunch, they split us into groups and took us on a walk around the place. This was a "walk," not a "hike." We can take a hike after the walk, if we want to. I probably wouldn't want to, but Ethan definitely does, and the other activities you can choose are a soccer game with Mr. Obester (that's where Javier will be), or boats that you pedal on the lake.

I might have wanted to do the pedal boats, but it's not warm enough to swim, and the lake isn't very big, and you have to wear life preservers and take a boat safety class first.

On our walk, the guide told us about all the nature we can see while we're at the wilderness retreat. You know, rocks and trees and insects and things. I asked if there are any bears, and she said almost definitely not. I asked her what she means by "almost."

Ethan, who hardly ever talks to anyone except me (and now my mom and dad), was asking a lot of questions, and once even corrected something the guide said that was wrong. She didn't mind. She was glad that someone else besides her is interested in nature.

All the hiking trails start at the same place. There's The Easy Trail, The Moderate Trail and The Difficult Trail. You can guess which trail I wanted to take. I thought I might at least be able to talk Ethan into The Moderate Trail, but no.

"Come on, Sean. You're strong. You're the King of the Pull-ups." That's actually true. I can do more pull-ups than anyone in the school, but you would never know it if you saw me. "It'll be an adventure."

I said yes, partly because I know Ethan still has his phone, and we can call for help. He's sure we won't have to, because he knows what to do.

They gave all of us bottles of water and healthy snack bars, and told us not to litter, then we all went to our activities or trails.

The Difficult Trail is difficult as soon as you start it. It goes up and up and up. Ethan says that's good, because we'll get through the hard part while we're still fresh. I actually don't feel that fresh. I'm not used to getting up so early on a Saturday, especially after a tiring week with Baxter and the bidding war and everything else.

There aren't many kids taking The Difficult Trail. So far we haven't seen anyone. Any people, that is. We saw a fox squirrel (which is more squirrely than foxy), a raccoon and a little family of deer. It was actually very cool. I got a nice picture of the baby deer before they all saw us and ran away.

I never saw Ethan so happy. He loves hiking, and he loves telling you all about what you're seeing. I guess Ethan was being his Uncle Neil and I was being him. I don't know if I'll remember everything he's telling me, but it's fun seeing how excited he can get about a bird or which berries you can eat.

Ethan had to pee, so he went into the woods, and I waited on the trail and looked around. It's so quiet. I didn't realize how high up we hiked. Then I heard some sounds from behind me.

It was Doug and Myles, one of his football friends.

"Look what's here." That's what Doug always used to say when he saw me before he thought I could help the band get famous. Now he knows I can't.

"Where's your girlfriend, Rosen?" He means Brianna. He knows she's not my girlfriend. "Are you lost on the mountain, you little _____?" (not a nice word)

I didn't know what to say, so I didn't say anything.

He walked over and stood close to me. I hate when he does this.

"Oh, does little Sean want to go home? I see a shortcut."

I looked where he was looking. It's a steep part of the mountain behind the trail where I was standing. If someone pushed you, it wouldn't be good. You might not fall all the way to the bottom, but you'd definitely crash into a lot of rocks.

Myles laughed. "'Fifth Grader Killed in Hiking Accident.' Oh, that's right. He only *looks* like a fifth grader."

Doug moved even closer to me. Close enough to push me off the trail. "They'll probably find you. Sooner or later."

"Hey, Doug . . ." It was Ethan. Doug and Myles were surprised to see him. I was, too. I didn't hear him walk up. How can someone as big as Ethan move so quietly? "I want you to meet my friend."

I moved away from the edge of the trail, and Ethan took his hand from behind his back and pulled out a really, really big snake. You could tell it was alive, because it kept moving its long, slithery body around.

Ethan held the snake near Doug's face. "Say hello to Doug . . . Poison."

The snake wiggled his tongue and made a scary sound. It was the only sound you could hear. Doug couldn't move. He looked like he was going to die of fear right there.

Then Ethan said, "They'll probably find you. Sooner or later."

The snake made that sound again.

Myles grabbed Doug and pulled him away. They ran down the trail together.

Ethan was still holding the snake. I didn't get too close.

"Um . . . Poison?"

"Oh. No. She's not poisonous."

"She?"

"Yeah. The females are bigger and a little meaner. It's just a hognose snake."

"Did you have it in your backpack, or . . ."

"No. She was on the ground. You pick them up with a forked stick. I just brought her back to show you."

"Thanks. Excellent timing, Ethan. I hope Doug brought that extra pair of underwear."

chapter 40

I got a picture of Ethan holding Poison before he let her go. The rest of the hike was nice. The trail ended at the top of the mountain, and you could really see a lot, including the soccer game and the pedal boats on the lake.

I was glad when we got back. I had to go to the bathroom, and after meeting Poison, I didn't really want to go in the woods. Ethan is going to take a shower. I looked at the showers. They're in the same building where the bathrooms are. It's one big room with like 20 showers and no shower curtains. Sorry. I don't think of taking a shower as a group activity.

I don't love group activities. Maybe it's because I'm an only child, but I actually need to have a little time by myself every day. I guess it's what I'm used to, and after a whole day of being with other people, even just one other person and one snake, I like to be alone for a little while.

That's a little hard here, because there are kids in our cabin and kids everywhere you look. I could probably be alone on The Difficult Trail, but I had enough hiking for today, and that's a place where I *don't* really want to be alone.

I remembered that there are some chairs on the porch outside the mess hall, so I took the book I'm reading, and I went there. It's quiet, with just the sounds of people inside getting dinner ready. I read for a little while, then I went back to the cabin to change.

It's getting a little cool out, and after dinner we're having a campfire. I don't know if a campfire keeps you warm or not. Ethan would know, but he isn't around. Maybe he's collecting non-poisonous berries for dessert.

After that long hike, and forgetting to eat my snack, I was really hungry. Javier sat with Ethan and me. He had fun playing soccer, which he calls fútbol. His team won, as usual.

I showed him the picture of the snake, but I decided not to tell him the whole Doug story. I don't really like when kids tell me things about other kids, so I usually keep my mouth shut. About other kids, I mean.

Becca, a girl I don't really know (except I sort of know everyone from working on the yearbook), came over to our table.

"You're Sean, right?"

Javier said, "Right."

"Wait." She looked confused, then said to Javier, "*You're* Sean?"

"No. I am Javier. I am very happy to meet you."

She looked at him for a second, then said, "Whichever of you is Sean, here." She put an envelope on the table and walked away.

I opened the envelope. There was a note inside.

Dear Sean,

*I can't text you because they took your phone,
so I'm writing to you on this cute stationery from
the B&B. I know I'm supposed to be helping with the
yearbook pictures, but I just can't be at that place.*

*Maybe I'm a little more upset about you-know-who
than I thought.*

Sorry. See you back in civilization.

♥ Bri

"Amigo, how do you do it? All the pretty girls
like you."

"No they don't." If he knew that Brianna
offered to kiss me and I said no, he would kill me.

When I finished eating, I walked around the
mess hall taking pictures. I skipped Doug's
table. I took pictures of Becca, and Brianna's
other friends because I know she'll want them in
the layout.

After dinner, everyone walked down to the other
side of the lake for the campfire. It was already

burning when we got there. The fire *does* keep you warm, at least a little bit, and it's really pretty. Everyone sat on these benches made of logs that were in a circle around the fire.

Ethan would only sit in the back row, because if he didn't, he'd block the view of everyone behind him. I sat with him there, and I stood up every once in a while to take pictures. Then I could see everything.

People from the wilderness retreat talked for a while about the history of this land, and the people who used to live here hundreds of years ago. Then we heard drums. Then these two guys came in and did a dance around the campfire. I liked it, but it lasted a little too long.

Then they brought out a big box of sticks, and we all toasted marshmallows around the campfire. I like watching them turn brown, but I don't actually like *eating* marshmallows, so I cooked mine and dropped it in the garbage when I was done.

After marshmallows, we sat back down, and some of the kids started yelling for the ghost stories, which the handout said is part of the campfire. The guide from the walk got up and told us that a few parents called and requested that we skip the ghost stories.

Kids started yelling, "Who? Who?" but she wouldn't say who it was. I know it wasn't *my* parents. Not that they love ghost stories or anything, but they would never call the school or the retreat to tell them what not to do.

"So instead, *you're* going to be the entertainment. I know that someone brought his guitar, and maybe he knows a song we can all sing." Some people groaned. I was one of the groaners. I don't really like sing-alongs.

Then someone came running to the campfire area. I think it's one of the dancers. He handed a piece of paper to the guide, who read it.

"Is there someone here named Sean Rosen?"

I can't believe it. I'm in the middle of the wilderness, and this is still happening. Everyone went crazy, pointing and making noises. I said to Ethan, "At least I don't have to sing along."

got up and followed the dancer guy.

"Did I do something wrong?"

"I don't know. Did you?"

I guess we're going back to the other side of the lake.

"Have you worked here long?"

"Too long."

He had a good flashlight. I was glad, because this place is DARK. I had *my* flashlight, too, but it's like a toy flashlight.

"How often do you do that dance?"

"Depends. Two to seven times a week."

"What does it depend on?"

"What the group pays for."

"Really?"

"Really. Did you have one marshmallow or two?"

"Um . . . one."

"For two, your school pays more."

"Actually, I only *wanted* one."

"Some schools have *no* marshmallows."

"Interesting."

I think the hike with Ethan today was good for me. I'm not scared being out here in the wilderness. I know. I'm walking with someone who knows where he's going. But I actually think I could get back by myself with my toy flashlight. "How did you get this job?"

"This job got *me*. It's my family's place."

"So the guide . . ."

"My sister."

"And the guy who welcomed us?"

"My father."

We're just coming up to the mess hall. That car looks just like my mom's. Wait! There's my mom and dad. What happened? I ran over to them.

ME:	Thorny?
DAD:	No.
ME:	Mary Lou?
MOM:	No.
ME:	Baxter?
MOM:	Nobody died. Was Baxter sick?
ME:	No. What are you doing here?
MOM:	Sean . . . there's a lot to talk about, and we don't have to do it all at once, but . . .
ME:	You are *not* getting a divorce.
MOM:	No. We're not.

My dad looked over at the owner's son, who was standing there watching us. Then he looked up at the owner, who was standing on the porch of the mess hall, also watching us, with someone who was probably his wife, or his sister.

DAD: Seany, let's just get in
          the car.
ME: Are we leaving?

My mom pointed to the backseat, and she and
my dad got in the front. I opened the door and
started to get in. What? There's a man sitting in
the backseat wearing a suit and tie.

MOM: Sean, this is . . .
ME: Hank Hollywood.

Oh my God. It's him.

MOM: Mr. Hollywood said you two
          hadn't met.
ME: We hadn't. He's famous. I
          know what he looks like.
          (then whispering) Do you
          know who he *is*?
MOM: Yes, Sean. We've been in
          the car with him for the
          past two hours.

DAD:	Here's what's happening, Seany. We're driving to a restaurant near here. Mom and I are gonna eat. You and Mr. Hollywood are gonna sit at another table and talk.
ME:	Like we did that time with that producer.
HANK:	Let me guess. You were six.
DAD:	It was just a few months ago.
ME:	And he wasn't a real producer.
HANK:	I'm glad I meet your standards.

I can't believe I'm in my mom's car with Hank Hollywood. Wait!

ME:	Is this a dream?
DAD:	No, Seany. We're all really here.
ME:	(to Hank Hollywood) Did you get our address from my

website?

MOM: Yes. He did. Did you know it was public?

ME: I didn't, but then Ethan told me. I made it private as soon as I found out. Sorry. I was trying to save money.

No one said anything else for the rest of the ride, which fortunately, was only a few more minutes. We drove up to a place called Kountry Kitchen. There was a black limousine parked in the lot.

ME: I thought you drove up together.

DAD: We did. But we're leaving separately.

We went inside.

DAD: You two sit there. Seany, we'll talk to you later.

chapter 42

Hank Hollywood pointed to a chair. I sat down, and he sat across from me. A waitress came right over.

HANK: Coffee and apple pie.
ME: That sounds good. I mean the apple pie. I'll have milk.
WAITRESS: You want the pie heated?
HANK & ME: (at the same time) No.

The waitress left.

ME: You look exactly like your
           pictures.

HANK: You sound exactly like your
           podcasts.

ME: You actually came to Pine
           Tree Wilderness Retreat.

HANK: *This* part I wasn't
           expecting.

ME: What do you mean?

HANK: I went to your house.
           I thought it was one of
           your parents.

ME: *What* was?

HANK: The person having those
           ideas. I thought they were
           just using *you* to get us
           interested. "Here's an idea
           from a 13-year-old."

ME: *That* would get you
           interested?

HANK: Yeah. If it was good. We
           want 13-year-olds to see

our movies . . . to see our
TV shows. Maybe a 13-year-
old knows what they like.

ME: Maybe he does.

HANK: (laughs) It took me about
           five seconds with your
           parents to figure out I was
           wrong. They didn't know
           anything. Why didn't you
           tell them?

ME: I was going to. I almost
           did a bunch of times. I
           guess I was waiting until
           I was sure it was real.

HANK: And you already had Dan
           Welch to help you.

ME: Right.

HANK: He's quite a manager.

ME: I know.

HANK: Nice to meet you, Mr. Welch.

ME: What do you mean?

HANK: Come on.

ME: When did you know?

HANK: Not for a while. You're
        good.

ME: Thanks.

HANK: You don't need compliments
        from me. You know you're
        good.

ME: I don't exactly know.

HANK: That's very true, Sean. You
        don't know. You *can't* know
        how good you are. Because
        so far, all you have are
        ideas.

ME: Well . . . I'm actually
        writing a screenplay.

HANK: But you haven't actually
        written a screenplay. A
        whole screenplay. Big
        difference. That's why you
        turned Stefanie down, right?
        You want to write it
        yourself.

ME: Right.

HANK: Then why are you wasting

	everyone's time with this
	bidding war?
ME:	How do you know . . .
HANK:	I work in a very small
	town. Word gets around
	fast.

The waitress brought us our pie. We both ate some.

ME:	I'm wasting everyone's time?
HANK:	Yes. You are.

It hurt my feelings to hear that.

HANK:	It happens to almost
	everyone in the business
	at some point. It happened
	to me. It's hard to resist.
	It's so seductive. "Everyone
	wants me. How much will
	they pay to *get* me?" But

in *your* case, it doesn't
matter. You don't want to
just sell the *idea*. You
want to write the
screenplay. No one will
pay you to do that. Because
you've never done it. So
getting them to bid is just
an ego trip and a waste of
everyone's time, especially
your own. Stop negotiating
and start writing. Finish
that screenplay. Then we
can all see if it's any
good. If it is, we'll all
want to buy it. *Then* you
can have your bidding war.

He stopped and drank some coffee.

HANK: Does "Dan Welch" handle
          everything for you?

ME: Yeah.

HANK: (he looked at me and laughed) *I* thought it was funny when we figured it out. Not everyone's going to feel that way.

ME: Are you gonna tell people?

HANK: No way.

ME: Did you tell my parents?

HANK: About Dan Welch? No.

I looked over at my parents eating.

ME: Are they mad at me?

HANK: I don't know. I don't know them. I like them.

ME: Yeah. Me too. Exactly *what* did you tell them?

HANK: That you emailed my office and tried to sell me some ideas.

ME: That doesn't sound so bad.

HANK: Oh, you like my pitch?

	Coming from you, that's a great compliment.
ME:	You never got back to us about *Electro-Pup*.
HANK:	To "us". You're funny. I *love* that Dan Welch only gave me a week. (looks at his watch) I'm not too late, am I?
ME:	What do you think of it?
HANK:	*Electro-Pup*? It could be very good.
ME:	I know.
HANK:	Or it could be very stupid. Having done this for 30 years, I can tell you that the odds are it will be stupid.
ME:	But in those 30 years, you never worked with *me*.
HANK:	Sean . . . Sean. I *was* you. Not quite *you*, but a version of you. I rented

out my comic books to
other kids. I organized
my neighborhood and put on
shows in my backyard. I
got things published in
magazines. I bought my own
movie camera when I was 14.
I always knew I wanted to
do this. And I knew I
wanted to do it in a big
way. I also grew up way
outside of Hollywood.
(he laughed) If *I* ever
tried calling the head of
a studio when I was *your*
age, my parents would have
seen Los Angeles on their
phone bill, and I would
have been busted. It's a new
world. We're clueless about
what our kids are doing on
their computers.

ME: How about my big idea?

HANK: No. Don't say a word about
         it.

ME: I know why.

HANK: Why?

ME: Because you don't want to
         pay me for it. You want to
         figure it out and get it
         for free.

HANK: Is that what you think?

ME: Yes. Why else would you
         send all those spies? Who
         was that girl at my school?

HANK: An actress. She's starring
         in one of our series next
         season. She's 23. Did you
         see her? Beautiful girl.

ME: I heard.

HANK: You thought I was trying to
         steal your big idea?

ME: Yeah.

HANK: Just for the record . . .

You do, in fact, *have* a big
idea?

ME: Yes! If you just answered
that first email . . .

HANK: You would have no way
of knowing this, but
Sean . . . I couldn't even
show that email to our
lawyers. They would kill
me . . . I'll repeat
that . . . KILL me, if they
knew I was talking to you
right now.

ME: Why?

HANK: You are a lawsuit waiting
to happen.

ME: What do you mean?

HANK: Some 13-year-old writes to
the Chairman of a multi-
billion dollar, multi-
national, publicly traded
corporation, saying he has

	an idea that will revolutionize the entertainment business.
ME:	And . . . ?
HANK:	So say you tell me this idea of yours. DON'T! And we decide that for whatever reason, it's a bad idea.
ME:	It isn't, though.
HANK:	Okay, let's say it's a *good* idea, but we decide, for whatever reason, that we're not gonna use it. Then, for the rest of your life— let's say another 80 years— we live in fear that in the process of doing what we do—you know, entertaining the world— we'll come up with something great, and suddenly Sean Rosen will

pop up and sue us, saying,
"That was *my* idea!" And
because I let a seventh
grader tell me his idea—
which I didn't. DON'T!—I'm
gonna *lose* that lawsuit, or
at the very least, spend
a gajillion of my company's
dollars *defending* that
lawsuit and/or paying a
gigantic settlement to you
and Dan Welch and your
imaginary law firm. You
don't have a lawyer, do you?

ME: I tried to get one, but no.

HANK: I knew it. You do your own
legal work, too. Anyway
Sean, that's why I'm here.
I had to meet you. If
anyone asks me, I *never*
met you. I'm *dying* to know
your idea-DON'T TELL ME!-
but I can't. Sorry.

Now all I want to do is tell him my idea. It would only take a minute. But I won't.

ME: Are you saying I can never
         work with a big company on
         this idea?

HANK: If you were already working
         with a company, maybe.

ME: Like on *Electro-Pup*.

He looked at me and smiled and shook his head.

HANK: Okay, Sean. Your parents
         probably want to get home.
         Here's what I'll do. I'll
         tell our TV comedy
         development people to try
         to make a deal with you
         on *Electro-Pup*. I'll leave
         that to them and Dan Welch.
         I don't know if they'll be
         able to, because it sounds
         like your Mr. Welch is a

tough negotiator.

ME: What about *you*?

HANK: What *about* me?

ME: You're supposed to be a shark. The shark that scares all the other sharks.

HANK: Yeah?

ME: No offense, but you don't seem that scary.

HANK: Not now. Not here at Kountry Kitchen. Not at the meeting no one's ever gonna hear about.

ME: Okay.

HANK: Back to business. You or your representative will negotiate with my people, but here are the rules: Your parents will have to know about it. They'll have to read the contract and sign the contract. If we

	make a deal, you have to keep going to school. We'll work around your schedule. Got all that?
ME:	Yeah.
HANK:	And remember . . . it's work. Even if you're really good, it takes time. You're going to keep having new ideas because that's who you are, but you have to pick one at a time and work on it. Because if you don't finish things, you're just another guy with ideas. To succeed in this business, you have to bring an idea to *life*. Show it to an audience. Have the audience like it so much they want more. They hardly ever do. The only reason

I'm sitting here is your
podcasts. You had an idea,
and you made it happen.
You have a style. You did
it well, and you did
it more than once. You
originated something and
you saw it through. Your
parents told me that
they're not involved at all.
You do it all yourself.

ME: My friend Ethan started
helping me.

HANK: Good. You're learning how
to collaborate. I'm leaving.

ME: You really don't want me to
tell you the big idea?

HANK: I really don't. And I
really do. Good-bye.

He shook my hand. He stopped at the cash register, gave the person a fifty dollar bill, said good-bye to my mom and dad, and left. I sat there

for a second and finished my pie. My parents came
over to my table and sat down.

ME: Are you mad at me?

They looked at each other.

DAD: (to Mom) You want to go
first?

MOM: Am I mad? No.

DAD: *I'm* not mad.

MOM: But I don't think we know
everything. Do we?

ME: No.

DAD: Do we *want* to know
everything?

ME: Probably not.

MOM: Was this all about that
movie you're writing?

DAD: The one you told my *mother*
about, but not *me*?

MOM: Or *me*.

ME: No. This was another idea.

	Well, two other ideas.
DAD:	You kill me. Get in the car.
ME:	Are we going home?
MOM:	*We're* going home. You're going back to your seventh-grade trip.
ME:	No.
MOM:	Yes. It's only one night. Why? Did you have a terrible time today?
ME:	Actually . . . no. It was kind of fun.
MOM:	See? This is *you*, Sean. This is how you are with new things. You're afraid you're not going to like it, and at first you don't, because it's new, but then when you give it a chance, you end up liking it.
DAD:	You avoid new things, but you write to the head of _____. And he actually

	shows up. You kill me.
MOM:	We know you like to have your own projects. And this can keep being your own project. But you have to promise to come to us if you're in trouble.
ME:	Define trouble.
DAD:	Use your judgment, Seany. We trust you. Make us want to keep trusting you.

chapter 43

I got back to camp just in time for milk and cookies at the mess hall before bed. Everyone asked me what happened. I said, "I can't really talk about it. But everything's okay."

Ethan walked back to the cabin with me.

"Is everything *really* okay?"

"Yeah. It's great, actually."

"Good."

And that was it. No more questions.

I got in the sleeping bag. So much just happened, and I wanted to go over it in my head for a little while, but one second I was lying there thinking what a relief it is that my parents finally know what I'm doing (more or less), and the next thing I knew it was morning. Breakfast was the best meal yet. I'm glad I came to Pine Tree Wilderness Retreat, and I'm glad I stayed.

On the bus ride home, I told Ethan my big idea. It sounds like it might be a long time before I'll be able to tell Hank Hollywood or any other big company. I never told anyone, and part of me was worried that after all this, when I finally *did* tell someone, they would laugh at me and explain in ten seconds why it will never work.

Ethan thinks it'll work.

When I got home, I went to Dan Welch's email account. This was in the inbox.

To: Dan Welch Management
From: Dan Welch

Hey Juice,

Anyone ever call you that? I got a couple buddies who do. You know, like Welch grape juice.

Hey, heres the person that wrote that email.

ashley._____@_____.com

I know. I shoulda told you before. I like u and Sean both, and I guess i just wanted to be in bizness with you guys. This felt like my 1 and only chance. Sorry.

If you see a collectible on the site that you like thats under 30$ let me know and its yours. For free I mean. Tell Sean that too. Its my way of opologizing. You just pay the shipping.

Im not always a jerk, i swear.

DW

I'm glad he sent us that, even though we already have Ashley's email address. I understand why

Collectibles did what he did. Like Hank Hollywood said, someone in show business wanting you (even if it's the wrong you) is pretty exciting.

My Dan Welch got to work.

To: Stefanie V. President
From: Dan Welch Management

Dear Stefanie,

I brought your very generous offer to Sean, and as usual, he said, "Stefanie is the best." My client has finally made a decision. He's not going to sell the idea. He's going to finish writing the screenplay.

I know. We're back to where we were a few months ago. When Sean finishes *A Week with Your Grandparents*, which I hope will be soon, I promise you will get to look at it first. As you said, you were the first one to push your button, and you never stopped believing in the idea. We hope you'll believe in the screenplay, too.

Sean and I like you and respect you, and we're both really sorry if we wasted your time. As you know, Sean is new to the business, and he's just learning.

I hope to send you his screenplay very soon.
Best,
Dan Welch

He sent the same kind of email to Ashley, though he didn't promise *her* she could see the screenplay first, too. He thought about it, but he didn't do it.

Okay, I'm closing out of Dan Welch's email account. I'm closing out of the internet. I'm opening up the screenplay and getting to work.

acknowledgments

I have a lot of people to thank: my panel of experts, Jeremy, Jordana, Chiara, Aurora, Melinda, Savannah, and especially Simon and Will; Christoph Niemann and Paul Zakris for the look of the book; Edgar McIntosh, Cameron Brindise, Jean Mancuso, Trish Soto, and the English department, PTA, and students of Ardsley Middle School; Bennett Ashley, Paul Lucas, and Stephanie Koven at Janklow & Nesbit; Tim Smith, Patty Rosati, Tu Anh Dinh, and the entire team at Greenwillow/HarperCollins, with extra-special thanks to Virginia Duncan, my great editor and publisher; my grown-up advisors and supporters, especially Jody Abzug, Rikki Abzug, Margery Davis, Denise DiPaolo, Maggie Gordon, Ruth Kaplan, Louise Kramer, John Levy, Lisa & Tony Manne, Tracey Moloney, Barbara Moon, Marcia Nasatir, Merrill Rose, Bobbie Sampson, Leslye Schaefer, Donna & Steven Schragis, Amy Schraub, Beth Merrifield Vance, Victoria Westhead, and Ken & Jackie Winston. I'll always be grateful to Julie Just, and, for their constant caring counsel, Lisa Baron, Karen Levinson, Kerry McCluggage, and Gary Carlisle.